SNAIL'S PACE

SUSAN MCDONOUGH-WACHTMAN

Cover design copyright © 2023 by Niki Lenhart
nikilen-design.com

Published by Water Dragon Publishing
waterdragonpublishing.com

ISBN 978-1-959804-37-6 (Trade Paperback)

10 9 8 7 6 5 4 3 2 1

*For my Dad, Francis Michael McDonough (1924-2010).
Thanks for the title.
I miss you.*

SNAIL'S PACE

1.

T HE YOUNG WOMAN mincing along the dusty track that passed for a street in the Hong Kong of 1884 did not look like an adventurer. From her dirt-covered button shoes to the parasol tipped over her head, she looked like what she was: a Victorian lady. But in one gloved hand she clutched a newspaper with three advertisements circled, and in her heart she clutched an unladylike determination.

She entered the doorway of the business that had placed the third of the advertisements she had noted in the paper. Less than five minutes later she emerged, the proprietor's laughter following her into the street. "No woman'll clerk for this business this day, lassy — or next year or next century!"

"Bloody fool," she muttered to herself. At least he hadn't suggested that she apply to a saloon as her previous prospect had done. But to suggest that she could only be a governess! Did she truly look such a milksop as that? Pausing to consider her reflection in a shop window, she supposed that she did indeed. Her perfectly piled chestnut hair and her carefully tended hands indicated that she should be sitting in her mother's parlor. Her mother, however, was long gone. She dismissed her unlamented mother from her thoughts. Perhaps her need for a life beyond the norm showed in her mouth — her wide, easily laughing mouth which she had inherited from her father. Her very much lamented father ... She hastily dismissed this thought also as tears threatened. What was she to do now?

She was startled from her dilemma by garbled speaking nearby. Looking around, she saw a Chinese gentleman dressed in a red silk robe who appeared to be addressing her. "I am so sorry, I am afraid I have no Chinese."

The gentleman was fiddling with a strange pendant which hung around his neck. She was shocked when a clear voice speaking unaccented English snapped, "This cursed thing! May the gods piss on it!"

She took a hasty step back and debated whether to run. The gentleman straightened up, then bowed.

"Excuse me, I have a proposition for you."

She looked around. No one else seemed to have noticed the strange behavior of the odd little man. She knew she ought to walk briskly and firmly away (she could hear her mother's voice telling her so), but she was intrigued.

"You are Miss Susannah Maureen Chambers McKay, aren't you?"

"How do you know my name?"

"I represent someone who wishes to hire you."

"Hire me? What can you mean?"

"You are looking for a job, aren't you? Almost out of money? No way to get back to England?"

Susannah gasped. This was too frightening. "Excuse me!"

She tried to push past him, but he didn't move, and she found that she couldn't push him aside. He was much stronger than he looked. At any rate, the curiosity which her mother had considered her most reprehensible trait drained her resolution.

The Chinese gentleman continued: "My employers are willing to pay you 10,000 fenigs a year, and, of course, include room and board. After one year they would deliver you to the destination of your choice. In return, you will instruct Intlack, the Eldest, in the customs and culture of the British Empire." The small man seemed to relax a bit. "That's what they want, although I did my best to talk them out of it. The job isn't an easy one, but you certainly won't be bored. You could say it will be an adventure, should you choose to accept."

The word caught her. The whole situation was unreal, but … *Adventure.* "What are fenigs?"

When he explained that "the major portion of a fenig is gold" because "they like the shine," Susannah's fears washed away in a tide of greed. "I'm sure they could be exchanged in England, if that's what you have in mind," he assured her.

A fenig must be some Chinese coin she had never heard of, she thought with wonder — 10,000 pieces of gold! She would be set for life — and never have to listen to the laughter of a shopkeeper again. "Who is Intlack?"

"The son of the house. He's about twelve, the way you'd reckon it."

"Where do they live?"

"On a ship. We'll be traveling a lot."

Susannah smiled. She loved to travel. Living on board ship with her father had been the happiest years of her life. This must be a very rich Chinese family! No doubt they had made their fortune in opium. Her father had said that many had. She looked at the tall ships docked in the harbor, weighing her options. They were pitifully few.

The man shuffled uncomfortably. "Look, you're not seriously considering this are you? I thought you'd turn right around and run away from me. I was counting on it, actually. You can't conceive of — these are aliens, you understand? They're from out of this world! The ship is in space!"

"I understand," murmured Susannah, although she had barely heard him. Her mind was full of adventure. Governess to a Chinese child. An alien indeed, but what a challenge! Living on a Chinese ship, worlds away from the English parlor she had hated. Perhaps the first European ever to experience the private life of a Chinese family — and the opportunity to teach them the civilized ways of England. No businessman in Hong Kong was going to hire her. She had clerked for her father, but no other man was going to give a woman such a job. She would have to hire herself out to an English family as a nanny or a governess — or do this.

She looked down at the Chinese man. "When do we leave?"

"Are you serious?"

She nodded.

"You're out of your head." He handed her a contract. "You sign this, we leave now."

"Now?"

"Now. My employers don't waste time."

Susannah began reading through the contract, while the Chinese man tapped his foot impatiently. Susannah glanced at him. "Sir, what is your name?"

"Chiang."

"Just Chiang?"

"That's it."

"Well, Chiang, what is a Shill?"

"It's what they call themselves."

"Hmm." *It must be another Chinese word I've never heard of,* Susannah thought. What a great deal I have to learn! Growing impatient with the foreign terminology, she skimmed the rest of the contract. She found the reference to the 10,000 fenigs and the guarantee to deliver her to her destination of choice after one year. "Very well," she said, tilting her chin up with what her father had called her "make full sail face."

Chiang handed her a writing implement and she signed her name. She assumed that she would now go back to her rooms to pack her luggage. But, no. Chiang spoke into the pendant hanging from his neck. "Beam us up, Snotty!" he said, and Hong Kong disappeared from Susannah's sight.

She flapped her hands wildly, off balance and terrified. Where was she? This ship, if it was a ship, was unlike any she had ever sailed upon. She stood on a platform in a small, brilliantly colored room. The process by which she had gotten there had been an indescribable experience, which she was trying not to remember. Apparently alarmed by her white face, Chiang put a hand to her elbow. Susannah wondered if she should allow a Chinese man to assist her in this way. She was not accustomed to dealing with brown-skinned people on an equal basis. She had no time to consider the problem, for a large purple creature stood at the desk in front of her, waving something in front of its huge, grotesque face and making loud honking noises.

Susannah gasped, "Is it speaking to me?"

"No, he's sneezing. He's allergic to us — he's allergic to all humans." He smiled at her. He seemed to be enjoying her bewilderment, his brown eyes sparkling. "I told you this would be different from anything you've ever experienced. Shall I take you back to Hong Kong?" He leaned toward her as though tempted to sweep her off her feet and carry her back himself.

She suspected that he could do it, too, in spite of his small stature. She straightened her spine.

"Certainly not." Her mother had always said that a lady should never show shock ("Unless, of course, my dear, it concerns something of a — well, something to do with, that is — of a sexual nature — and then it would be far more appropriate simply to faint.") Susannah felt a little bit like fainting now, but then the sense of humor that her mother had always described as "unfortunate" began to stir. What would her mother consider appropriate behavior when confronted with an allergic alien? Susannah smiled graciously at the snorting creature.

Chiang, however, looked disappointed. "Well, I'll take you to your room, then." He led her out through a turquoise curtain. "You can spend some time getting adjusted. Tonight at dinner you'll meet the Family."

She took two deep breaths and followed him into a corridor hung with more of the brilliantly colored drapery. This was certainly nothing like her father's ship. If only fate could have allowed them to make this voyage together, how much he would have enjoyed this! She blinked back the tears. When she was alone, she would allow herself to cry a little. She had not had much opportunity to grieve. Finding a means to eat had seemed more crucial.

Chiang noticed her blinking as they walked down the corridor which swirled with color. "It's a little overpowering at first, isn't it? With the Family, color is stature, the brighter the better. And the Family, you must understand, is very important. Here we are." He pushed aside a magenta curtain and ushered her into a room. She sighed with relief to find that the draperies here were muted pastels. "As you can see, you're being put in your place right off."

"It is reminiscent of the Arabian Nights!" Susannah fondled a soft curtain. "It is fortunate that I have been put in my place; I do not believe I would rest at all with colors as brilliant as those we saw in the corridor!"

Chiang was fiddling with a curtain at the side of the room. He pulled out a small bundle and gave it a snap. She stared in astonishment as it inflated immediately into a softly padded bed. "When you want to deflate it, just squeeze it at either end."

Susannah felt the bed. It was soft and springy and felt as though it was filled with something more than air.

"Feathers," said Chiang. "Believe it or not. They discovered goose down mattresses on Earth."

She turned sharply at that. "So — please be frank. Where are we, Mr.Chiang?" She faced him squarely, noting that he had the compact, muscular look of many of the Chinese she had seen. *Was* he Chinese?

"Just Chiang, please." His brown eyes contemplated her curiously. "I'm not sure. Probably past Venus by now. Want me to ask them to turn around?"

She turned away from those probing eyes. "You did inform me that we would be traveling on a ship that sailed in space. I — I surmise that I did not entirely conceive..."

"There was really no way for you to comprehend it. I knew this was a mistake. I tried to tell them."

Susannah didn't hear him. Something had just occurred to her. "Are my employers — Chinese?"

He stared at her. "No!" He sighed and swung his arms in frustration. "I thought I had made that clear. I told them you were from the wrong culture for this. No exposure to alien life. Not even a conception of other worlds."

She heard that. "What do you mean? Are you suggesting that I have had no exposure to alien life? Just what words would you use to portray the difference between the Chinese way of life and that of an English woman? Can you not conceive that after growing up with my mother in London, Hong Kong was like another world to me?"

He snorted. "Honey, you don't know what alien is. I told them, 'If she doesn't go into shock, she'll go stark, raving crazy.' But they didn't listen."

His tone annoyed her. "Are you not Chinese? From Earth?"

Chiang paused. "Well, yes. A long time ago. But please don't tell anyone. I tell everyone I'm Maurean. Earth is considered the backwoods of the universe — it doesn't even have a Universal Representative! I'd appreciate it if you kept my origins to yourself. If you want to be respected, you'll adopt a new homeland, too."

Slowly Susannah sat down on the low bed, then jumped up in shocked surprise. "Does it live?"

"Not exactly, no," he said absently. "Go ahead and sit on it. It won't hurt you."

But will I hurt it? she wondered. She sat down gingerly. The bed again began a soothing purr. Trying to relax, she watched curiously as Chiang fiddled with his small box. "Would it be rude to inquire the purpose of that?"

"No." He looked down at her with a frown. "I'm the only human on this ship besides you, Susannah." She knew she ought to reprimand him sharply for using her first name without permission, but it seemed a little inconsequential at the moment. "You can ask me anything you want to. Nothing is too rude. But you should only ask me, okay? You have no way of knowing what's rude to any of the other creatures on board. Some of the others — oh, this is ridiculous. You don't belong here. This —" he shook the box, "is a communicator, a translator, and several other things. And right now I'm going to communicate to the Captain and to the Family that they must take you back. They had no business bringing you out here."

She leaped to her feet again. "You'll do no such thing!" She grabbed his hand away from the communicator. "Who are you to make such a decision for me? To what should I return? I should go back to become a governess to a spoiled little English child? Knowing all the time that I could have been — been flying through space having extraordinary adventures instead? I will not!" She tried to soften her tone. "Please, Chiang." She realized she was still holding his hand and blushed, dropping it. "This will not be an easy adjustment, but it will certainly be an interesting one! Please. You did it!"

"Well, I, yes, I did, but — you don't —" He sighed. "Most women wouldn't even have come. Why did you?"

"Well, I needed the money. I believe you know that my mother died in England." He nodded. She suspected that he did not like looking up at her, so she sat down on the bed again. "And my father brought me to Hong Kong on his ship." She smiled. "It was his fond wish that I meet a likely gentleman and marry, and so be secure. But, alas — Well, to tell you the truth, I was not a bit saddened when no likely gentleman appeared — a few unlikely gentlemen, but I soon sent them packing! I am afraid I have a very unladylike appreciation for travel and adventure."

"So I'm learning."

"Yes, well. The fact is that when my father died, I found to my dismay that the ship was not his ship at all, but belonged to the bank. He was not, I fear, much of a business man. I had to get a job. I must admit being a governess was the last thing I wanted to do. But in my straitened circumstances options were few." She sighed. "It seemed that no one would hire me to do anything else."

"You must have relatives somewhere."

"Oh, yes, certainly." She tried to cross her ankles, but the bed was too low to do it comfortably. "In England. It would have been six months before they even heard of my predicament and could send for me. In the meantime, I had to eat."

"But why *this* job?" Chiang demanded with persistent disapproval.

"Because it paid more. I knew that if I took this job, I'd eventually be able to go back to England in style, instead of as a — an orphaned old spinster, or a governess, forever dependent on others for my survival. And, I must admit, my father was a gambler, and I may have inherited a propensity for the same." She smiled, remembering. "He lost it all in the end, but he did have a mighty fine time. My mother always disapproved of him. He was a charming rogue, and I believe he may have misled her when he courted her. She did her best to instruct me in the art of being a lady. Which most certainly was not easy for either of us! And she attempted to instill in me a caution which I obviously lack!" She laughed. "Father taught me that to live, one must take risks!" She tossed her head back, and a few pins slipped out of her hair. Cascades of brown waves threatened to descend unchecked. "Oh, fiddle! Is there a looking glass available?" The ship seemed slightly damp; like a London fog, it was making her hair curl.

"Behind this curtain." Chiang showed her how to hook the curtain back, displaying a blank screen. "Tap it once —" he demonstrated, "and you have a mirror. Tap it more times and you get other stuff — but I don't think you're ready for that yet. And behind this curtain is your tube."

"Pardon me?!"

"For your 'personal needs.' The toilet. The facilities. The water closet. Only there's no water. You'll figure it out."

"Oh," she said faintly, hoping he was right. *What would Mother say to this?*

"They keep everything behind curtains," he continued. "Except their thoughts." He glanced at her sideways, causing her to become aware of his slanted eyes.

Her father had called the Chinese inscrutable, she recalled. She stopped fiddling with her hair to frown at him suspiciously. Whatever could his comment indicate?

"I'll go see if dinner is ready," he said casually.

"What did you mean?" she demanded.

"Mean by what?"

"Do not play the innocent with me. You said, 'Except their thoughts.' I am not an imbecile. What did you mean?"

"No, you're certainly no imbecile. Our employers are telepaths. They don't speak aloud," he continued, seeing she didn't understand. "They can read minds. But they're very discreet. They only read surface thoughts — for conversation, you know. They won't look any deeper — unless they 'hear 'something that might be dangerous to them. So think peaceful thoughts and the rest of your brain will be your own."

Susannah sagged a bit. "Oh, my goodness … I-I may have been hasty in saying nothing would dissuade me from remaining aboard! Could you describe the Shill, please?"

"They like colors and jewelry. They don't like violence or disagreements of any kind. Except between the Regisax." At her questioning look he explained, "The Regisax are the ones who handle the machinery on board. Their species has done this for the Shill for generations. I guess the Shill can handle the hot tempers and narrow mindedness of the Regisax because they're so used to it. The only thing a Regisax cares about is his pride and his machinery. If the one you met — whom I call Snotty, because he's allergic to me — to us, I mean — if he could read my mind, he would have torn my skull open with one finger claw long ago. The Family could not run this ship without them. The culture of the Shill is about fifty times older than ours — that is, than that of the Chinese, which is older than you English will admit — and they live about five times longer than the average human. Their children take about forty of our years to mature. Your charge is only twenty-five."

"But — what do they look like?"

"Oh!" He grinned. "They look like snails, my dear. Like great, *big* snails."

2

W HEN SUSANNAH ENTERED the dining room with Chiang, she found that the Family were the most colorful snails she had ever seen. Their shells were dyed with every color imaginable and inlaid with sparkling jewels in intricate patterns. Their bodies, however, were like any other snails' — greenish-gray and damp with slime. The dampness in the air which she had noticed earlier was far more noticeable in the dining room. Looking at her host, hostess and student-to-be, Susannah understood. She swallowed hard and hoped she'd be able to eat. Three pairs of tentacles swung toward her, weaving sinuously. She caught the edge of an excited thought:

[The barbarian has the color of a lowest of the low/world-bound mud-crawler of no color, Mother! What can such a one teach me?!]

A repressive feeling followed: *[Manners!]*

[But she is thinking that we are — wet and sticky, I think — is that polite?]

[This is not the Earthwoman's accustomed form of communication. She will learn. As will you.]

[But, Mother!]

A new thought-voice interjected sharply:

[Intlack!]

Susannah stumbled slightly at the strength of that voice in her mind. (Also, her best shoes were pinching her toes.) Having the thoughts of another creature in her head was a disturbing experience. If one could not call one's thoughts one's own, then what was left? She was diverted, however, by the realization that the personalities of the "speakers" came through as clearly in her head as they would have done had she heard their voices — perhaps more clearly. Intlack "felt" to her very much like her cousin, James, whom she had occasionally been forced to share a schoolroom with when she was young.

[Father! The alien is thinking of me as like unto a member of her Family! This I cannot bear!]

[Hush!]

The force of the thought was enough to make Susannah wince. Chiang chuckled as he guided her to the round table, which was elaborately laid and barely raised off the floor. The two large snails' shells reached about as high as Susannah's chin, the smaller one's to her waist. They were — sitting? — next to each other around the table, with two places left for herself and Chiang. Large pillows had been provided for the humans.

"Susannah-Teacher," said Chiang with great formality. "May I present Simtlack-Diplomat, his mate, Cheetlon-Consort, and their son, Intlack-Eldest."

The names and titles as she 'heard' them echoed by Intlack were slightly different, and she realized that Chiang's pendant was unable to capture the nuances. Trying to suppress thoughts about their squishy green bodies and sinuous tentacles, Susannah curtsied to each in turn. She 'heard' a thought with the flavor of Cheetlon:

[I apologize for our little outburst as you came in, Susannah-Teacher. As you can feel/sense/receive, our son is in need of your guidance. My mate/love/friend and I don't spend the time with him that we ought.]

Chiang gestured for her to sit. She sank, rather awkwardly, onto the cushions. He sat cross-legged with practiced ease.

"Thank you, Sir and Madame, for inviting me here."

[Thank you for coming,] came Simtlack's overpoweringly strong reply. *[I hope you will find the adventure you were hoping for. (Chuckles?)]*

Intlack's tentacles were pointed steadily in her direction, but she caught no thoughts from him.

[Don't stare, dear.]

The tentacles swiveled away, then irresistibly wove their way back again.

[Do you slime/crawl/leave a trail?]

"P-pardon me?"

Chiang snickered.

[Intlack! The Teacher is of the same species as Chiang and has the same habits.]

"Well," said Chiang, "more or less."

Susannah frowned at him. "You could do with a lesson in deportment yourself," she snapped.

"Please, teach me, O Refined One!"

There was the equivalent in her head of a throat clearing.

"Please pardon us," said Susannah, chastened. Then she projected the thought as clearly as she was able: *Pardon us.* Intlack's tentacles were pointed steadily in her direction, but still she caught no thought from him.

[You must speak, or Chiang-Adviser will be unable to hear you. I am afraid you have not the strength of thought for him to receive you.]

"Oh, yes, of course," murmured Susannah. *And a good thing, too.* "I still do not comprehend," she said aloud, "how you learned of me?" She wiggled uncomfortably on the pillow, tugging her dress down over her ankles. It was not merely modesty; surreptitiously, she undid some of the buttons on her shoes.

The self-assured thoughts of Simtlack told her:

[We heard of you from our reppresentative in your sector of space. We had told all of our representatives that we wanted a

Teacher/Companion/Friend for our Eldest. We preferred someone of an alien species, someone who would be able to teach him some tolerance and some manners, as you can sense he needs. We reviewed reports from a variety of sectors and chose you. We chose Chiang, for obvious reasons, as the best of our advisers to make contact with you. He will be your adviser until such time as you feel at home here.]

Cheetlon interjected gently: *[May that time come soon. I'm sure it must be burdensome for someone of your independent spirit to be so dependent upon a male of your species to whom you are not bonded.]*

Susannah tried to take a breath. The understanding of Cheetlon, though an alien, and the incredible sensation of having another being in her head was beginning to overwhelm her. Trying to distract herself, she looked down at the (of course) colorful table. Differently colored portions of what appeared to be gelatin puddings, liquids and leaves were arranged in patterns on the low table. She tried to think of some way to thank Cheetlon for her kind thought.

[There is no need,] Cheetlon assured her.

Susannah started. When would she remember that words were not necessary here?

[The accustomization will come. The food is all safe for humans, Teacher,] Cheetlon added. *[And it is necessary for us to eat Now.]*

There was a distinct change in the mental atmosphere. Simtlack lowered his tentacles, and the other two Shill followed suit. Susannah looked doubtfully at Chiang, who gestured to her to lower her head.

[We give thanks,] thought Simtlack, *[gracious thanks, Oh Master, for sustenance, life, color. Thanks for the safe arrival of Susannah-Teacher. Keep our shells strong and our bodies soft in your service. We expose ourselves now, Oh Master, trusting in you to protect and keep us. We ask your mercy.]*

Solemnly Simtlack moved forward , leaving his shell behind. Susannah tried desperately to clamp down on her nausea as the other two snails crawled out of their shells. Beautiful shells! Beautiful shells! (Slimy worms! Slimy worms!) They crawled up onto the table and planted themselves on the food. They made faint sucking sounds as they moved. Susannah swallowed.

She looked around the table. How was she to eat? Slurp off the table? Her mother had always said, "When in doubt as to the precise use of a dining utensil, watch your host." Susannah felt hysterical giggles rising.

"Here you go," said Chiang cheerfully, handing her a spoon and a small tube. "Let's eat!" Susannah looked at the tube blankly, then looked at Chiang. He placed the tube on the table and sucked. Then he winked at her. "It's called a straw."

Cautiously she placed the tube on the table and sucked. "Why, it's apple juice!"

"Close enough," agreed Chiang. He pointed with his spoon. "Water, milk of a sort, wine, ziltlur and others you wouldn't know." He picked up a spoon and began scooping the food off the table. The snails crept slowly forward on the table. Were they replete when they all reached the center?

"Are they listening to us?"

"Probably not. They're pretty single-minded eaters. They won't speak again until the meal is over."

Slowly, Susannah scooped up a spoonful of pink gelatin, trying not to watch the Family. She sampled the gelatin cautiously, then with pleasure. The taste was faintly reminiscent of Turkish Delight. She scooped up some more.

"You shouldn't eat dessert before dinner," admonished Chiang. "Try this." He pointed at a swirling mixture of green leaves and yellow pudding. She dipped cautiously, trying to keep one of the leaves on her spoon. "Just grab it," advised Chiang, taking a leaf with his fingers and stuffing it into his mouth.

She looked at him with horror, but — it did look good. She sighed and picked one up. She would have to explain to Cheetlon about forks as soon as possible. The leaves were minty and the pudding was like a meat gravy. She finished all that was in her immediate vicinity.

"Let's drink to your new life," suggested Chiang.

She looked down at the table, where the liquids were bound by more solid foods, wondering which to choose. She watched Chiang as he applied his straw to the purplish swirl he had called *ziltlur*. Awkwardly she copied him, sucking up the strange liquid which tasted like sweet water until it hit her throat, where it began to warm up, until it hit her stomach, where it seemed to explode. "Whoo!"

"That's ziltlur!" He said it proudly. "I requested it. They —" he pointed at the snails, whom she had succeeded in ignoring for a few moments — "drink nothing more potent than apple juice. But they don't mind if others indulge." With a flourish, he placed the tip of his tube on another pool of the bright purple liquid. "Ah!"

Potent — did that mean that she was drinking spirits? She stopped abruptly, shocked. Her mother would never have allowed her to drink spirits! Even her father had told her to avoid them: "Liquor can release all your inhibitions, honey bunch, and that's dangerous enough for a man, but could be deadly disastrous for a woman." So, she was doing something doubly forbidden. She had never before done such a thing. Slowly, she drank some more.

The initial disappointment of the taste was more than offset by the thrill of the conclusion, she decided. And she was finding it less disturbing to watch her hosts on their slow circuit around the table. There were smears of gelatin and liquid left behind each one. Their tentacles were pointed at their meal. Truly, they were not so repulsive. Merely snails. She had never been bothered by the small snails of Earth. Whyever should she be disquieted by enormous snails on a spaceship? She chuckled to herself.

"Better watch it," said Chiang. "Don't drink it too fast." But he was still grinning as he said it.

His grin reminded her of the Cheshire Cat. Would he disappear finally, leaving nothing but that grin? She scooped up some of the pink dessert, but found it tame after the ziltlur. She craved more of the drink, but elected to heed her father's warning. She certainly had no intention of becoming inebriated in the company of her new employer! The whole extraordinary experience — leaving her home and boarding a spaceship, being employed by these aliens — and dining with them! — was more than she could ever have fancied — an extravagant romance. She was marvelously fortunate, she told herself, to have such an opportunity to learn about an alien culture, and perhaps educate them a little about her own. After all, she was an Englishwoman! There was a great deal that she could teach a snail boy — and his parents, no doubt, as well.

"Are you finished?" Chiang straightened up, putting down his spoon and straw.

She looked at him through blurry eyes. He was really a fine looking person, for an Asian. His skin was smooth, and a lovely almond color. His hair was dark and silky. She had never really become acquainted with a foreigner before. Her mother had been afraid of anyone who was not white — anyone, in fact, who was not English upper class. But her father had enjoyed the company of all sorts of people, and he had told Susannah many stories when her mother had not been within earshot.

"Well," said Chiang, startling her. "Are you ready to go?"

"But — but what about —" She gestured to the Family.

"Oh, they'll be eating for hours yet. They don't eat often — only about once a week, Earth time. It's a big occasion for them."

"Oh." She took a last sip of ziltlur. It would be a great pity to waste it, and Chiang had said the Family did not imbibe.

"That's enough, I think," said Chiang, rising gracefully to his feet. "I don't want to have to carry you back to your room. Something tells me you may be one of those people who can't hold her liquor." He put a hand out to her, and she reached up to him, intending to imitate his graceful swoop upward.

However, the heel of her unbuttoned shoe caught in her skirt and the shoe slid sideways, as did the pillow, as did she, causing her to miss Chiang's grasping hand. She swung her arms out for balance, Chiang made a wild sweep for her, and both of them splattered full length onto the table, narrowly missing landing on any of the Family. Liquid and gelatin flew everywhere, splotches of bright goo splurted onto the already brilliant tapestries and tile floor.

Susannah lay stunned, her face in what appeared to be chocolate pudding. She tasted it. It didn't taste like chocolate pudding. It tasted like kippers, which she didn't like.

"Blistering suns! Susannah, are you all right?"

[By all the —]

[Has the Teacher expired/dehydrated, Mother?]

[No, dear.]

Susannah wondered how much longer she would be able to lie with her face safely hidden in the table. She turned her head slightly, hoping for something tasty. Ziltlur! Happily, she slurped.

[Chiang! Can you please explain this?]

"Sorry, sir, she tripped. She may have had a little too much ziltlur."

[Hmph.]

[What's tripped, Mother?]

[And did you, too, have too much ziltlur?]

"No, sir! I tried to catch her."

[Well, if you're able, perhaps you could remove her. You know we can't stop our meal now. The prayer has been said, the service begun.]

"Yes, sir. If you'll just go on with the service, sir, I'll get her to her room right away."

Cheetlon's gentle thought suggested: *[I think perhaps a trial period would be in order, my dear.]*

[Yes,] boomed Simtlack. *[Chiang, you have one non-consuming period to instruct her. We cannot have incidents like this.]*

"Yes, sir. Susannah, can you walk?"

A hand touched her elbow. She licked up the last of the purple fluid, then turned her head. A brown, red, blue and green face peered down at her. She felt hysteria bubbling up.

"Are you all right?" Chiang tugged her to a sitting position. They were both covered with multi-colored slime from head to foot. A blob of red gelatin slid off Chiang's ear.

Susannah began to giggle. "Are you aware that you have verra many colors yourself now? So you do!" She was surprised to find her father's faint lilt appearing in her speech.

Chiang grunted and hauled her to her feet, his thin fingers tight on her arm. He half-supported, half-dragged her off the table. She glanced back to see that the Family was ignoring them, once again moving slowly about, digesting the now miscellaneous stew on the table.

The sight inspired her to a further outburst of mirth. "Whyever d'they bother with all the pretty, pretty patterns when they jus slurp, slurp, slurp it all up regardless?"

Chiang pulled her out of the room, hampered at every step by her slimy, sodden skirt. "Why do women of your culture wear so much clothing?"

"Yer not grinnin' now," she commented. "'Stead of the body leavin' the grin behind, the grin's left —"

"Will you be quiet?"

"You did think me a fine funny woman before, did you not?" she asked with as much dignity as she could muster as he half carried her down the hall. "When I didna know the first thing about what to expect, you thought that was quite a fine joke. I believe that it is quite the appro—appropra— quite right for you to lose your grin now, so I do."

"I take it that means no."

"Did you know that there is yellow gelatin upon your head? Yellow gel, yellow gel, yellow —"

He stepped away from her. She staggered and collapsed on the floor, chuckling. He stepped around her and grabbed the end of her skirt, then dragged her off down the hall feet first, leaving a colorful, slimy trail behind them. She glimpsed it as they turned the corner into her room. *I'll have to tell Intlack,* she thought. *I can make a trail.*

3

W HEN SUSANNAH WOKE UP the next morning, she thought she was inside a rainbow. She sat up, and immediately the bed began to purr. She leaped from it, not quite able to believe it wasn't about to grab her or eat her, and was relieved when it stayed where it was.

She looked down ruefully at her stained and crumpled dress. What was she to do for clothing? Well, whatever it was, she could not wear this! She was afraid she could not continue to wear black in this culture in any case. Mourning for her father would have to be suspended early.

Forgive me, Papa, she prayed. *But you understand, I am certain. I have little enough status here as it is.* She took off her gown and stood in her undergarments, considering the draperies. Perhaps she could do something with them for the time being ...

"Susannah?"

"Chiang?"

"Can I come in?"

"You wish to enter my bed chamber?"

"You want me to yell through the door?"

"But it is — not proper for —"

"This is not England."

"No. I … Wait until I find a — I don't have any — any raiment." She blushed and lifted the bed covering.

"You mean you don't have any clothes on?" A diaphanous robe was tossed at her through the curtained doorway.

She considered it with dismay, reluctantly pulled it on over her underthings, then supplemented it with some of the bedclothes. "Well … You may enter."

Chiang entered and surveyed her for a moment. She could not fathom his expression. "How do you feel?" His robe today was a deep purple with scarlet trim. His brown eyes seemed to be taking in all too well the precarious state of her dress.

She heaped the bedclothes up around herself a little more. "I feel very well, thank you."

"That's good. I was afraid I hadn't gotten the yamlit down your throat soon enough."

"The — I beg your pardon?"

"Yamlit. A post-drink remedy to keep you from feeling the aftereffects of too much liquor."

"Too much liquor! A lady never becomes inebriated!"

He folded his arms across his chest. "And I suppose it's normal for you to fall on the dining table."

"I've been a tad clumsy since I turned thirteen."

"Clumsy!" he snorted. "Do you remember coming back to your room last night?"

"Well, in a manner of speaking …"

"So," he said sarcastically, his robe swishing as he straightened up, "I suppose you've also been forgetful, 'in a manner of speaking,' ever since you turned thirteen."

"Perhaps so."

"Perhaps you could have cost me my job!"

"I am not aware that I have any responsibility whatsoever in regards to your job!"

"I'm responsible for seeing that you know how things go around here, and dinner is a big deal to them!"

"Well, you did not explain that to me!"

"Exactly!"

Susannah blinked. "Oh."

Chiang turned his back and muttered, "I'm not denying that I've failed you. Now you know why I didn't want you to come in the first place. I don't want the responsibility."

"Why did you not simply explain to Simtlack you did not want to be responsible for me?"

He looked at her broodingly. "Simtlack doesn't accept refusals from his employees."

"Well, then, resign from your position."

He stamped his foot. "You just don't get it do you? This is not Earth. These are aliens. I am under contract to Simtlack to play a certain role. He's a fair employer, and he's paying me very, very well. But if I try to break that contract, I might not survive."

"Oh, surely you exaggerate. Simtlack appears to me to be a perfectly civilized creature — for an alien. Could you not take him to court or — or something of that nature?"

"Oh, you —!" Chiang spluttered and swung around as if to leave, his robe flying. He flipped back around and yelled, "This is not a democracy! The Shill are the representatives of an Empress who governs this whole sector of the universe! Your puny little empire on Earth boasts about how the sun never sets on the lands ruled by the Queen — well here it is the *suns* which are ruled! And all the planets which accompany them! Simtlack is the territorial governor for this quadrant! He has unlimited power here!" He clapped his hands with frustration. "Think of it this way. You're an Indian woman in India —"

"I am not —"

"Please put aside your provincial prejudices just for a moment. Imagine yourself a native. You've done something to offend Her Majesty's Lord Whosit, who is visiting from London. What do you think will happen to you?"

He stared at her, brown eyes hard and challenging. Susannah sat down on her bed, which purred. She said slowly, "They would most likely put me in prison — and worry about what to do with me at a later date."

"Now you're getting the idea. And you and I have offended Simtlack by our behavior last evening."

She looked away, trying to take it all in. "So what recourse have I now?"

"We'll have to wait and find out what he decides." He sat down next to her. "Do you regret staying?"

She looked at him soberly. She touched her hair, frizzy from the slightly damp air. She looked around at the pastel curtains and breathed in deeply of the faintly musky scent of the ship, and the even fainter scent that Chiang used. She petted the bed as though it were a cat, and it rumbled in response. "How could I regret experiencing such wonders?"

He shook his head. "You really are far more than I bargained for. I was so sure I'd be able to get you to quit right away. Especially when you found you'd have to accept me as an equal."

"Whatever do you mean?" But she couldn't meet his eyes.

"Just look how hard it was for you to contemplate being an Indian woman. Were you even able to admit to yourself you had a hard time dealing with me?" He shook his head.

"I do trust I have not done anything to offend you."

"Hah! Listen to yourself! I do trust that after all these years with the Shill I have a thick enough skin to deal with prejudice! I've heard some pretty uncomplimentary things from Intlack!"

"I can imagine, I —" she stopped, silenced by Chiang's raised hand. Was he listening to some announcement she could not hear?

Idly she imagined what her mother would say if she were with her. ("Allowing an Asian man in your room — and sitting on your bed! This is totally unacceptable behavior. I have never been more shocked!") *Oh, but Mother, I'm sure you have only to wait for even greater shocks to come!*

Chiang lowered his head and sighed. "Well, that's that."

She waited a moment, then bounced impatiently. "Stop it, Chiang. Tell me now."

He grinned. "Simtlack has decided to call it a nihilism. That's not their word, of course, that's a vague translation." When she stared at him blankly, he went on. "What it means is that the incident never happened."

"It? What 'it'? You mean my unfortunate clumsiness last night? We just pretend the incident never happened?"

"We pretend, but they don't. As far as they're concerned, once it's declared a nihilism, it's gone, memory banks swept clean. When you belong to a race which reads minds as easily as we sneeze, you have to have some protection against inadvertent 'slips of the tongue.' Of course, your episode was a little more than that. But apparently Simtlack has decided to give you the benefit of your inexperience. Never, never refer to the episode again. it would be a far, far worse indiscretion for you to mention a nihilism than it was for you to fall on the table in the first place." He stood up. "Oh, and he also has placed you on a trial period. One week, your time, more or less."

"One week! But Chiang, what does Simtlack think I can teach Intlack?"

"I believe he was hoping for manners, but now he has his doubts, hence the trial period. You may have noticed Intlack is a little outspoken. Not a good thing for a diplomat's son. Intlack is supposed to be attending state dinners with his parents, but they have had a couple of unfortunate incidents."

"Were they declared nihilisms?"

"No. The problem with a nihilism for a Shill is that they learn nothing from it." He tapped his head. "All forgotten. Simtlack did not want to declare Intlack's little problems nihilisms, because he wanted Intlack to gain the experience."

"This must all be very difficult for Intlack," she said thoughtfully.

"I s'pose." He shook his head. "I thought when you'd met Intlack, you'd reverse course in a blip."

"Chiang — how do you suggest I go about teaching him?"

"I thought you had no doubts about your ability to teach."

"I find I have many more doubts about myself today than I had yesterday."

Chiang's breath whooshed out. "Well, thank the stars for that. Maybe now you'll be a little cautious." He shrugged, obviously not hopeful. "Normally a Shill youngster is allowed to grow pretty much unencumbered by discipline of any kind until it's older than Intlack is, but ... I suppose your first job will be to earn Intlack's respect. To the Shill, you have no caste. You'll have to convince him that you have something to teach before you'll be able to get anywhere."

"Well, I know you consider my ability questionable, but I am rather anticipating the challenge."

He snorted. "If there's one thing I've learned in the short time I've known you, it is that you enjoy a challenge."

She smiled, thinking how deceptive his small form was. She had bruises on her arm from his grip the night before.

"Perhaps because you're too ignorant to be frightened by the challenges you're facing," he added.

Her smile disappeared. "Well, thank you very much!"

"You are welcome. My room is the next cubicle down. You are welcome there. In between us is the bath we share. You are welcome to use it. Please do not wander. You are liable to be very unwelcome in other places."

Susannah's brain had stopped two sentences back. "A bath? A bathing tub, do you mean? How wondrous! But I — I am a little uneasy about privacy here. It's disconcerting enough to know my thoughts can be heard, but to know that anyone can come into my room at any time is very —"

"Yes, yes, I know. It would be the greatest of scandals for anyone to see you unclothed." He snorted again. "There isn't much I can do except recommend that you either grow used to it, or try to train everyone to your custom. I don't know which will be the more attractive challenge for you. And before you say it," he held up his hand, "I hereby pledge to always call out for permission before I enter your abode. Or the bathing room, just in case you're using it," he added.

"Thank you. Don't they find it noisy with no real room dividers?"

He tapped his head. "Not the Shill. No ears, remember? They have no concept of sound as we know it. The Regisax are too wrapped up in their own concerns to pay any attention to other noises, and I guess the others have just grown accustomed to it as I have."

"How many others are there? How many species?"

"Oh, I'm not sure, half a dozen maybe. I've never counted. Any other questions?'

"When and how may I acquire more clothing?"

He grinned. "Is it really necessary? Don't look at me like that!" He held up his hands in mock alarm. "You frighten me! I'll take you to the seamstress after breakfast. That should be fun."

When Susannah was sure that Chiang had gone, she rose and dumped the bedclothes behind her, then used her unique chamber pot. Chiang had been right; she had figured it out without difficulty. Pleased with herself, and much more comfortable, she brushed aside draperies until she found her looking glass. She regarded herself in shock. Her appearance was that of a dance hall girl! She had never actually seen a dance hall girl, but ... she had to get some new clothes immediately! At least all the color ought to help her relations with Intlack. She looked thoughtfully at the walls. Surely not quite so many draperies were needed. She pulled a couple of them down. To her relief, they pulled easily and didn't tear too much. She decided to start from scratch. Slinging the draperies onto the bed, she unwrapped her nearly-transparent robe, and removed her undergarments. She wondered if it would be possible to wash them.

There was a rustling at her "door." She turned and gasped to see Snotty — or someone who looked like him — entering, carrying Intlack on a huge silver platter. She grabbed up the diaphanous robe and wrapped it around herself.

[White as a Tanvia worm! Intlack's thought came through to her clearly. Bleah! Well you should wrap yourself up in enchanting drapery, although you have no standing/Family/caste. Why did you wear dismal wraps yesterday like an outcast slave?]

Snotty snorted and bared his teeth in what Susannah took to be a grin. She clutched at her slippery cover. "Why you rude little slug! Who do you think you are, barging in here? And then insulting me? Remove yourself at once, and don't come back in unless I say you may!"

[Who am I? Who am I?] Snotty's eyes widened as he caught Intlack's furious thought. *[Who are you that you speak to me thus, you peon from an inferior world where the only creatures anything like the One Tribe Which Dwells are mindless miniatures which your people have the gall/nerve/incivility to eat, you —]*

"Enough! Enough! Get out!" Susannah advanced, but they didn't move. She looked around wildly, then picked up her bed and began swinging it. Snotty protectively lifted the platter higher, his eyes screwing up as she approached. "Get out!" she yelled.

[No! Intlack's tentacle stalks were stiff. You should slither for a million years without your shell before me! You should —]

Susannah hit Snotty with the bed using all her strength, and he stumbled backward into the corridor. Susannah threw the bed after him. Intlack was still broadcasting in a hysterical mind-shriek when Snotty began to sneeze. Intlack's screech became a scream that caused Susannah to grab her head. She heard the platter crash to the floor and Intlack's furious order to Snotty to hold his arm level. Peering through the curtain, she saw Intlack clinging to Snotty's arm with his long foot, while the Regisax tried unsuccessfully to stop sneezing. Intlack ranted at Snotty to reenter her room, but Snotty, eyes streaming, turned and shuffled off down the hallway, Intlack still clinging to his arm.

4.

S USANNAH PULLED AWAY from the door after Intlack had left, grasping at her slipping negligee and breathing hard. "What a little — worm!" She thought of Intlack on Snotty's arm and giggled. Poor little worm, his great, childish dignity all gone. She began to laugh, then sobered as she heard footsteps pounding down the hallway. She was unsurprised when Chiang tore through the drapery door.

"What ... did ... you ... do?"

She swallowed hard, striving to recover her own dignity. "I — I gave Intlack his first instruction in deportment."

His intense gaze bore into hers. "In what way did you instruct him?"

"Well, I — He was extremely rude! He entered my room without knocking, and he immediately proceeded to insult me! What choice had I but to chastise him?" She tried to look contrite. "I am deeply sorry if I have offended again."

Chiang took a deep breath. "Please. Just tell me exactly what you said to him."

She fiddled with her filmy coverings. "Well, it was very distressing, and I may have been a bit outspoken."

"Surely not. Not you! Go on." He waited.

"I believe I told him to — umm — remove himself, and I informed him that he must ask permission before entering my room in the future."

"Well, that doesn't —" He narrowed his eyes. "You're not telling me everything. Intlack was furious. Everyone on the ship could hear him."

"Oh. Well. I was quite perturbed myself ..."

"Yes?"

"Yes, indeed, and —" she finished with a rush, "— I do believe I called him a worm, and then he left." She smiled.

"You called him a —" Chiang turned a sickly tan and looked around for a place to sit down. "Where?" he croaked. "Where is your bed?"

"My bed? Oh, yes, I recall." She looked out in the hallway. "Here it is!" she called cheerily, and dragged it back into the room. His eyes begged for an explanation. "I am most penitent for losing my temper. I have a most unfortunate tendency to throw things when I am enraged."

His brown face turned beige. "Buddha preserve me. You threw your bed at Intlack." He sank onto the bed.

"Actually, I threw it at Snotty. So," she added briskly, "is there something I should do now in order to expedite the process of apologizing?"

His mouth dropped open. "Process?"

"Well, certainly. For instance, if I offended an acquaintance in England, I would call on her and leave my card, perhaps some flowers, and she perhaps would pardon me, or perhaps refuse to receive me, and then —"

"Susannah. Please. Stop. This is not England. Intlack is not your girlfriend." He stood up and his voice rose. "Intlack is an *alien.* What's more, he is the son of your *alien employer.* More than that, your employer is *the* most powerful *alien* in this *quadrant*! I *thought* we had *discussed* this! *You — you —*" He stuck and choked, then picked up her bed and threw it across the room.

"I see you have the same unfortunate tendency as I," she murmured.

"*You will be lucky to live!*" he bellowed. "You *certainly* won't be allowed to *stay* —"

They heard Snotty's heavy tread in the hall. "They're here," said Susannah.

Chiang hissed, "Do you want to know how the Family kills people?"

Susannah turned to face the door, her head high. Snotty's steps halted. Then they heard him leave. Then came Intlack's thought-voice:

[You requested that I acquire permission before entering. May I enter?]

Chiang's furious eyes opened wide.

"I would be honored to admit you," said Susannah, holding the torn curtain aside for him. "I must beg your forgiveness. I was overhasty in my response to you earlier."

[I am told that I was — discourteous — to you also. Forgive me.]

The force of his thought made her head ache. As nearly as she could tell, he was looking at the ceiling. Then his tentacles swiveled toward the open mouthed Chiang.

Chiang coughed. "Excuse me, Intlack-Eldest. I–I was just instructing Susannah-Teacher. I will depart."

[Yes. And do a better job from now on.]

"Yes, Eldest." With a beseeching glance at her, Chiang hurried out.

Susannah decided she needed to do her best to restore Intlack's wounded pride. Automatically, she smiled her sweetest smile, then realized that that would not be effective. How did one placate an alien male? Well, she decided, all males have egos. "I was greatly surprised to be visited by one of your stature so soon. You caught me unaware and unready, and in my nervousness, I was not courteous. I am most exceedingly sorry."

[As well you should be. And I —] He seemed to struggle for the concept. *[I also am regretful.]*

"Perhaps we can teach each other about courtesy in our cultures."

[I do not think there is much you can teach me. But I will try to be patient with you.]

She suppressed a smile. "Thank you."

He seemed to be listening for a moment, then said:

[I am told to inform you that your meal will be served when we are through communicating.]

"Oh, that is good news! I am ravenous!"

His tentacles swiveled down, pointed straight at her.

[We consider it bad manners to discuss bodily feelings.]

"Oh! Forgive me! And thank you for telling me." She followed him on his slow progress to the door.

[The servitor who brings your meal is unable to speak/think/ communicate. It will simply enter. Perhaps you can refrain from throwing anything at it.]

She couldn't tell whether he was intending to be amusing or not. "Thank you for telling me," she said again.

[We will communicate again after your meal,] he told her regally. *[Perhaps you will explain your idea/thought/concept of petting/soothing/placating an ego.]*

Susannah's eyes widened. When would she remember that he could read her mind?

Snotty was waiting for Intlack with the platter. Snotty bent down, and Intlack crawled on.

[You will communicate to me what is this ego?]

Susannah bowed. "Yes, Intlack-Eldest. I would be honored. Thank you for honoring me with your presence."

She could feel his satisfaction and relief at having his authority and pride restored in front of Snotty. Then Snotty turned and shuffled away. Susannah sighed gustily. *So much excitement, and all before breakfast!*

She returned to her former occupation — getting dressed. She washed herself off as best she could. She decided against washing her undergarments since she didn't know how to dry them. Wincing, she put the dirty things back on, then wrapped some of the draperies around herself, and finally donned the filmy robe overall. Surveying herself in the looking glass, she felt satisfied that she was decent, if not wholly respectable.

As she had expected, no sooner had she gotten the robe on, than Chiang burst through the curtain.

She regarded his reflection in the looking glass with annoyance. "I'm going to have to teach you some manners, too. Please knock, or — or some such — before you come in."

"What happened?"

She waved a hand, watching herself to see whether the filmy clothing showed any gaps as she did so. "He apologized, I apologized — we were very civilized." She looked at him out of the corners of her eyes. "Much as it might have been with my girlfriend in England. Although no flowers."

"He apologized?"

"Yes, he was quite sweet." She pulled the robe a bit tighter.

"He was sweet?"

"Yes." She noticed a movement behind him at her door drapery. "Could you step aside? I believe my breakfast servitor is attempting to get through."

He stepped back against the wall, and she watched with amazement as a somewhat dog-like creature walked in with a tray strapped to its back. Chiang unfolded a table and chair from behind a drapery, then lifted a second tray off the one strapped to the creature's back. He patted the creature on its perfectly flat withers, and it loped out of the room.

"'Like a tea tray in the sky,'" Susannah quoted softly to herself. "Will wonders never cease?"

"Pardon me?" said Chiang. He waved a hand for her to sit down.

"It is of no consequence," she said, feeling suddenly lonely. Would she ever again meet another being familiar with Lewis Carroll? "Won't you join me?" she asked Chiang politely. She was relieved when he declined. She didn't feel ready for another lecture. She sensed it had been a strategic error for her to sit down, however. She could see him straightening up, enjoying his ability to look down at her for a change. She braced herself for the homily to come.

"Aren't you going to apologize?"

"To Intlack? I did."

"To me. *To me!*"

"Whatever for?

"You *said* you'd be careful!"

"Well, I was quite circumspect, I think. I did not say nearly as much to him as I wished to." Her stomach rumbled. "Do you object if I partake of my meal?"

"Do what you wish. It is what you are best at. I am leaving. I have work to do." I'll return when it is time for you to go to the seamstress." He left.

Susannah enjoyed her meal very much.

When she was through she piled her dishes neatly on the tea tray and explored her room. There wasn't much that she had not already seen. *Well, now how shall I occupy myself?* she wondered. *Surely just a little exploring won't get me into trouble ... Chiang would be horrified,* she thought, as she peered cautiously out into the hall. She was undoubtedly being very foolish and was risking both of their lives again — or something to that effect. She told herself she would only go as far as the bathing area he had told her of.

She found it right next to her own room, as he had promised. She explored the fixtures and promised herself an all over just as soon as she had some clean, new clothing to put on. Then she thought she would just take a peek into Chiang's quarters, as long as she was there. As with her own, the walls were covered with draperies. She was disappointed. She had thought surely someone who lived on the ship would have personalized it somehow. She peeked behind a few of the curtains, but found nothing different from her own room. Feeling guilty and disappointed, she ventured out into the corridor again.

As long as she had come this far, surely it would do no harm to take a few more steps, just to see what was around the curve

... It was difficult to tell where doorways were, with every wall covered in filmy draperies. She ran her hand lightly along, probing for openings. When she found one, it took her by surprise, and she almost fell into the room. The opening was much larger than her own and Chiang's doorways, and there were a multitude of pillows strewn about.

"Excuse me? Is anyone present?" she called cautiously.

When she heard no sound, she stepped in. It gave her the impression of being a meeting room, with the pillows thrown about on the side where the door was, and a platform at the opposite end. She tiptoed over to the platform and ran her hand along the far wall. Something dark and shiny caught her eye. Was this finally a work of alien art? She pulled the curtain aside and gasped, immediately drowning in nothingness — the wall was one great window and she was staring out at empty space.

She sank dizzily to the floor and lay there breathing more and more quickly and feeling faint and sick. The stars were reaching out for her, trying to swallow her up. It was too immense. There was only a ship in empty space, and alien creatures who cared nothing for her, and no way to return to the familiar, safe world of her birth. *The stars are going to devour me with their cold uncaring unendingness ...*

With a snap the draperies were yanked over the window, and a brown face was thrust in front of her own. "Will you never learn?" He gripped her arms with angry strength and attempted to drag her to her feet, but she was shivering, and the tears trickled unheeded down her face.

Chiang said several things she didn't understand.

"Why couldn't you listen to what I said for once, you perverse, pathetic —" He tried to shake her, but she flopped in his hands, and he clasped her in his arms instead. "What a rock-brained, nosy, obstinate, prying, intractable, dull-witted —"

"Yes, that's sufficient," said Susannah suddenly, straightening up. "I perceive your intention. I was ill-advised to explore on my own." She turned away from him and pulled a crumpled handkerchief out from her bosom.

"Ill-advised! Ill-advised! You — You do not begin to describe it! You are so lucky you upset no one but yourself here! If you had chosen to go in the other direction you would be minced meat by now. The Regisax do not like humans at any time, and they certainly haven't formed a positive opinion of you! If you had wandered into one's room — I shudder to think!" And he did.

She giggled. "I believe I have disturbed you more than myself."

Furious, he stood up. "Let's go, it's time for you to see the seamstress now."

Her smile dissolved. "Oh, please, no, Chiang, I can't. I can't see anyone now. I need some time to —"

He grabbed her arm and this time he did drag her to her feet. "Can't? Ha! There is nothing you can't do. And I spent precious favors getting this old worm to see you right away. You see her now, or you'll be wearing that outfit for the next two weeks." He gestured at the robes, which had not weathered her recent crisis well. He leered at her. "Come to think of it, perhaps it wouldn't be so bad, watching you try to keep all that stuff on for a few weeks ..."

She pulled hastily away from him and drew the robe more tightly around her. "I will accompany you."

He grinned. "I thought you might." He led the way out of the big room. "Don't worry, you'll like her. A nice old Dorian silkworm. Only seven feet tall — very short for her species."

5

S USANNAH PUT DOWN her teacup with a sigh of relief.
[Feel better, dear?] The old silkworm's voice rumbled in her head.

"Oh, yes, much." Susannah looked around with enjoyment. It was the first room she had seen on the ship with draperies of only one color — a soft, pale green. Susannah found it marvelously refreshing.

[Nothing like a cup of tea to relax you after an upset ...] The Dorian put her own teacup in its saucer and rested her tiny hands on her segmented body. *[I didn't want to see you, you know. Chiang said I would like you, but I wouldn't trust that human (sorry, dear) — I wouldn't trust his judgment about —]*

"Pardon me?" Susannah drew her attention back from trying to figure out how the creature stayed in her chair. She was seven feet tall (or long) as Chiang had said, and her body was bent to fit the shiny oval seat. There was what appeared to be a knitted afghan spread over her "lap" and a tiny pair of spectacles perched on her — end? —below her tentacles. She reminded Susannah of the caterpillar in Alice in Wonderland. "Chiang said what?"

[He said I would like you. So, of course, I didn't want to see you. Susannah smiled at the thought of how summarily the seamstress had dismissed Chiang after he had introduced them. He bears out the old saying, "You can never trust a human." But I think you must be the exception to the rule.]

"Oh, thank you, but I did not realize there were any other humans on board."

[There aren't, dear, but there are a few roving around the quadrant.] Dory's thoughts chuckled in her head. *[Just enough for the rest of us to have developed a poor opinion of your species.]*

"Oh, dear. "Susannah contemplated this information with dismay.

[Not to worry, dear. As long as you're Intlack's Teacher you should have no cause for concern.]

"But how can people deceive you if you can hear their thoughts?"

[They can't, dear, but that does not stop them from trying. And of course some are shielded, and then, not everyone in the quadrant can practice telepathy. Would you like some more tea?]

"Oh, no, thank you. It's very good, though. What kind is it?"

[Mulberry.]

"How unusual," said Susannah, wondering what else the worm consumed.

[If you have questions about my biological makeup, dear, why not ask?]

"Oh, I am sorry! I did not mean to be rude!"

[Oh, stars. Don't worry about it. I've been around a long, long time, and I've heard much ruder thoughts than that!]

"I was wondering if you were related — in some way — to the Family."

[Well, not personally. Our species developed in the same solar system, and we share some characteristics. But we Dorians never had the ambition of the Shill.]

"Dorians?"

[You humans call us silkworms, but that's not accurate.]

"Thank you for explaining. I am afraid one characteristic of our species is unbridled curiosity."

[Now that is one thing I like about humans. You remind me of my children when they were just little pupae. Well, now, Chiang said your need is urgent.]

Susannah lifted up the miscellaneous veils which draped her. "All I have is what I'm wearing and what I wore when I came." She did her best to project a picture of her mourning dress.

[Oh, my, I see what you mean! Not designed to improve your status — or catch the amorous eye around here.]

Susannah laughed. "Well, I do not believe I wish to catch any eyes. I believe I just require to — blend in."

[Stars! A lovely female such as yourself should be thinking about a little twining!] The old worm clucked to herself and stood up, putting her afghan aside. She patted the afghan as she folded it over the arm of the vaguely egg-shaped chair. *[Isn't it lovely? A fine old Feestor picked that up for me ... from a human, I believe. The sort of work I could never do myself.]* She fluttered her tiny hands. *[I think I see what I want to do with you. We'll try it and see what you think.]*

Her voice chattered on in Susannah's head as a silky sheath began to grow around the lower part of Dory's body. It rippled with blue and silver, and Susannah gasped at the beauty of it and its seemingly magical appearance.

[You like it, eh?] The old worm's tone was complacent. *[This is for the party. I'm so undisciplined — I always make the fun things first.]*

"A party?" Susannah sucked in a happy breath — then let it out with a sad swoosh. "But I would not attend a party!"

[Whyever not?]

"But — I have not been invited."

[Silly human! Everyone's invited. The whole ship goes. That's one of the nicest things about the Family. They never discriminate about parties. The servitors take turns serving and partying. The rest of us just party! And this old worm does love a party. There

now.] With satisfaction she pulled the fabric gently away from her body and held it up to Susannah. *[Ahh! Right again! What a wonder I am!]*

"Oh, yes!" Susannah touched the shimmery stuff gently. "Oh, it is beautiful!"

Dory was already spinning another fabric around herself. *[I think I'll just make it very simple, a wrap-around and loop up sort of thing. Between you and the fabric, we don't need much else. I'll get my assistant right on it. Yorty!]* Her bellow was deafening to Susannah. A small, green creature darted in as she pulled another length of fabric off her body.

The creature, Yorty presumably, chattered and ran out again.

[I never heard anything so ridiculous. Yorty, you come back here. I don't care what Snotty said, she is not going to throw things at you. Dear, did you really throw a bed at that Regisax?]

"I am afraid I did."

[I wish I could have seen it.] Yorty came cautiously back into the room. *[I want this in the basic wrap. Do it right away. This one —]* she held out the blue and silver *[— set aside , and I'll oversee you when you work on it later.]* Yorty scampered out. *[May I suggest something, dear?]*

"Certainly!"

[I've heard that you are on a probationary status here ...]

"That is correct. Until the next Family dinner."

[I think that the best thing you can do, my dear, is continue to charm the Eldest.]

"Intlack? Charm him?"

[Oh, yes, you fascinate him. If you can win him over completely, no social blunders you make will matter. You'll stay. They refuse him nothing, you know.]

"I thought he seemed a little spoiled. Thank you so much for the guidance, Dory."

[Think nothing of it. Now, what else ... Oh, of course, I'll send along some underthings, too, dear. They may not be what you're used to, but you'll need something.]

"Oh, yes," said Susannah, blushing. "I do need some badly."

[I'll have your everyday dress and your underthings delivered after your next sleep period.]

"Thank you so much for taking the time to see me. I have certainly loved speaking with you."

[I've enjoyed it too, dear. Come see me again soon.]

"I will! Thank you!"

Chiang had come to collect her, but he barely paused when she came through the curtain before racing off down the hall.

"Still annoyed she made you leave, I presume?" said Susannah.

"I am not annoyed. I am busy. I will order you dinner — even though you've just had tea, I am assuming you are hungry again?"

"Well, yes."

"And then I will leave. I have a great deal to do. Can I trust you to stay in your room this time?"

"Would you procure me some books, please?" asked Susannah humbly.

Chiang paused and glanced back at her. "Books?"

"Yes, I do find time hangs a little heavy when I am alone."

"Hmph." They had reached her room. He swept the curtain aside for her, then entered and swept another curtain aside. "This is a multi-D screen."

"Pardon me? I thought that was my mirror."

"It's both." He touched the panel beneath and it slid open. Susannah was astounded to see that her reflection had disappeared. Chiang took a small box out of the opening and handed it to her. "This turns it on. This changes the program. This adjusts the volume. Keep it down."

"Keep what down?"

Chiang touched the "on" button. Susannah leaped back as sound filled the room and strange creatures suddenly appeared before her. "What are they?" she squealed.

"They're not real. They're — theater. But you don't have to pay for it and you can change it if you don't like it." He pushed her gently onto her bed, and closed her fingers over the box, pressing her finger on the program changer.

The creatures disappeared and a Regisax leaped across the floor. Susannah screeched and dropped the control box. The Regisax's prey appeared: a willowy humanoid with a glowing sword.

"I programmed it to English for you," said Chiang, but Susannah was not listening.

The sword threw off sparks as the humanoid swung it and it contacted the Regisax's long gray claws. The humanoid appeared to be losing the battle ...

Chiang departed.

•   •   •

Her second meeting with Intlack went much more smoothly than the first. Susannah sat on her bed facing him as he lay? sat? on the floor. In order to allay his resentment of being "taught," she decided to simply tell him about life on Earth.

In spite of himself, Intlack became intrigued by her stories. He especially liked anything that involved tricky talk and manipulative reasoning. Fortunately, she had plenty of stories to tell of her father's intricate business schemes, and her mother's equally intricate social ones. Of course, in order to explain the maneuvers involved, she also had to include a great deal of information about the culture. She was surprised to find that it was easier to explain her mother's social dealings. The dance of English society was not as foreign to Intlack as she would have expected. Susannah believed she was beginning to glimpse the reasoning behind Simtlack's choice of an Englishwoman as a tutor for his son. The subtle reasoning of a diplomat, she thought, as she told Intlack yet another story about her mother, was not dissimilar from the reasoning of a social-climbing matron.

"Since Lady Browning had neglected to invite Mother to her soirees, Mother began inviting Lady Browning's daughter-in-law to tea. After a few months, when Mother had gained the younger woman's confidence, she divulged numerous uncomplimentary remarks which Lady Browning had made about her son's wife —"

Intlack's tentacles were riveted upon her. *[Son's wife —
that is also daughter-in-law?]*

"Yes, sorry. So the daughter-in-law began revealing to her
husband these very rude utterances of Lady Browning, and in no
time at all, Lady Browning had no more influence over her son
than over the stable boy. Less, actually. This was devastating to
her. And then, Lady Browning somehow came to hear that Mother
had become a bosom companion of her daughter-in-law!"

[Ah!]

Susannah smiled. "Yes, ah! Mother's revenge was sweet
indeed when Lady Browning called on her and literally begged
her to help restore her relationship with her daughter-in-law,
and so, of course, with her son."

*[Were the confidences which your Mother divulged to the
daughter-in-law true words?]*

"Oh, indeed!" Susannah was shocked. "Mother never told
an untruth! Perish the thought! But, surely Intlack, your people
do not lie. They could not! Why do you ask such a thing?"

Intlack was shocked in his turn. *[No, my people could never
communicate an untrue word. But it is well known that humans
can and do. And ... it must be said ... we Shill can ... withhold/be
silent/be circumspect .... in our communications.]*

"Ah!" said Susannah in her turn. "I have wondered how it
was your people could engage in diplomacy. It would seem a
certain amount of — circumspection — would be required for
a governor."

*[A Shill with the strength of mind of one of my parents is
capable of communicating as much or as little to as many or as
few as he or she wishes,]* explained Intlack. He paused, then
admitted: *[I do not yet have that strength.]*

"No doubt you will, however," said Susannah soothingly.

Intlack's tentacles swiveled in what she was beginning to
recognize as his listening mode. *[I am told that your midday
repast is prepared.]*

"Oh, wonderful!" She caught herself before she said an
impolite word about the empty state of her stomach.

[But, of course,] Intlack caught her drift regardless. *[I do not understand this necessity to feed your body so often.]*

"I do not understand it, either. I just know it is necessary. That is to say, I do understand in a general way the physical reasons for my hunger, but I do not understand my bodily functions in detail."

[Physical reasons?]

"Yes. The way in which my body operates which causes me to desire sustenance. Do you not have a Science Teacher, Intlack?"

[Science?]

"Yes — that which explains why bodies operate the way they do, what it is which causes the world to go around —"

[The worlds going around is simplicity. But if you understand your body, why do you not change your metabolism so as to eat less often?]

"Well, I certainly do not understand it that well ... And, in addition, I truly enjoy eating!"

[So? Well, should you wish to change, it is simplicity.] He projected a confused (to her) jumble of pictures and instructions, including a few which nearly made her lose her breakfast.

"Please, Intlack! Your ideas are too advanced for me!"

[Yes! So! You admit it! You are stupider than I!]

"Gracious! I certainly do not admit any such thing! In some things I know more than you, and in some things you are more learned than I!"

[But my father knows more than I in all things.]

"But your father does not have the time to instruct you! And, naturally, you would never anticipate that I could possibly know as much as your father!" She smiled sweetly.

[No! Of course not!] His tentacles swiveled around. *[You have given me much to think on.]*

She did her best to suppress the thought that he was confused but would not admit it.

[I think you must have learned from your Father and Mother some diplomacy. Especially from your Mother. Yet, I feel that it is

your Father whom you more fully miss/mourn/regret. Is this perception accurate?]

She was surprised and touched by his attempt to understand her. "Well, yes! I — perhaps one day I could attempt to convey why this is so."

[Yes. And also to discuss with me the petting of the ego.]

She laughed. "Oh, yes. We did not discuss that topic yet, did we?" She smiled at him and realized with surprise that she was no longer repulsed by the sight of his shiny, gray body beneath the sparkling shell.

[And I am no longer disgusted by your dry whiteness — or at least, not as greatly. What does it mean when you stretch your mouth?]

"What do you hear when I do it?"

[I hear nothing. I feel — pleasure. As when starting a meal.]

"That is what I feel. How do you show pleasure?"

[On the outside?]

"Yes."

[We leave a trail.] He demonstrated by moving a few feet, leaving a slimy and shiny substance behind him. The tentacles swiveled up to her. *[You are sickened again.]*

Susannah looked away. "Yes. I am sorry."

[Why are you sorry?]

"Because ..." She tried to not to look at the floor. "Because it is a natural occurrence for you, and I should not make judgments about others based solely on what seems natural to me."

[But how else should you judge?]

She stared at him blankly for a moment. "That — that is true. But ... Nevertheless, I can learn to overcome and alter my judgments with the goal of becoming more tolerant."

['Tolerant.' This is ... accepting/allowing/enduring?]

"Yes. But most of all, accepting. I hope to become more open-minded."

[Yet, I feel that you have been wishing to close your mind to me?]

Susannah smiled again. "So I have. It must be very confusing. I will try to explain. I wish to close off from you what might be hurtful to you, and open myself up enough to empathize with you, so that I may understand what is hurtful to you and why. Does that sound sensible to you?

[No. Why have concern for my feelings?]

Susannah blinked. "Well ... It is ... polite ... to concern oneself with the feelings of others." She sensed blankness from Intlack. "It is also diplomatic," she added.

[Ah. This I can comprehend.]

"In addition to that — I am beginning to care for you!"

[This surprises you.] Intlack's tentacles swiveled around. *[This surprises myself, also.]* He moved towards the door. *[I must think on this. We are completed for this day.]*

She stood and bowed. "Thank you, Intlack. I have had a very instructive morning."

The tentacles pointed at her steadily, and after a long moment she heard: *[I also.]* Then he slid slowly out the door.

She could hear the silver platter being lowered, then the heavy tread of the Regisax going down the hall.

Turning, she noticed her floor. "Blech!" She hurried to the curtain which hid her strange little sink and looked around for something suitable to use as a rag. She couldn't find anything appropriate. Desperately she tore another curtain off her wall and used that, scrubbing and trying not to think about it. Pretty soon she wouldn't have any draperies left, she thought. And she wasn't even able to get the stuff off the floor.

6

S USANNAH WAS PLEASED a short while after Intlack's visit to see
the tea tray creature enter. Keeping her wits about her sufficiently
to converse with that young snail had certainly given her an appetite.
She took the tray from its back and set the tray on the floor, then,
somewhat apprehensively, she patted it as she had seen Chiang do.
Its skin felt smooth and soft. It immediately turned and left the room.

She shook her head and looked around, trying to remember
which curtain the table was hidden behind. She wondered if it
would be a dreadful breach of protocol if she were to pin all the
curtains aside until she had learned where things were.

She heard a subdued voice at the door: "May I come in?"

"Yes, certainly. So you have gained some manners, as well!"

Chiang stepped in, his robe swishing. He looked at the floor
with a frown. "What's that?"

"What is what?" She looked up from her cakes (they looked
just like fairy cakes — how wonderful!). "Oh, I see. Perhaps you
can tell me how that can be removed." She took another bite of
— whatever it was. "That is snail slime."

He was silent so long she finally looked up from her food to see what was wrong this time. He was still staring at the floor.

"He —" His voice came out a squeak. "He slimed? But that — that means he was delighted with you!"

"It was a demonstration." She took a sip of her tea.

"A what?"

"It is of no consequence. Would you like to join me? I feel very rude sitting here eating before you, but I am most desperately hungry."

"When are you not? I'll call a slimer for you."

"A what?"

"Well, there's all kinds of this stuff around when the Family has a party. So there's one creature on board whose only job is to clean up slime."

Susannah sat back from the table. "Similar to the tea tray?"

"The what? Oh, your servitor. Yes, similar to the servitors." He spoke into his box. "I've summoned the slimer."

If I am ever to be independent, I must learn very soon to do that, thought Susannah. "Do the Shill just train creatures to do whatever they need done?"

"They don't need to train them, they've bred them to do these things naturally. These creatures live to do what they do." He found another chair behind a curtain and sat down. He reached out for the drink pitcher, but she reached it first. He laughed. "I forgot. The woman serves, right?"

She paused. "That is the custom where I was raised. Is that incorrect here?"

"It is not usual most places. It's not usual on this ship. But it's a big universe, and

you can find most any custom you can imagine — and some I'm sure you can't — if you travel long enough." He waved to her to continue pouring, then picked up his drink. He turned his head at a slight swishing sound. "Here's your slimer."

"Doesn't anyone knock around here?" Then she saw that, like the tea tray, the slimer couldn't knock. The slimer was just an oblong spongy creature with no apparent sensory features at all. It propelled itself silently over the slime on the floor, then departed, leaving a clean floor behind. It was Susannah's turn to be silent with shock. Chiang smiled. "They — they breed them?"

"Yes, basically."

"It seems rather barbaric — to create a creature simply to serve your needs."

"What do you call cows? The Shill would consider it barbaric to breed something just to eat it."

"I suppose that is so." She pushed her plate aside and sighed with relief. "A civilized meal is a great comfort."

"You're amazing." He shook his head at her as he put his cup down. He leaned his elbows on the table in a way her mother would have rebuked.

"How so?" She piled things neatly on the tray, taking comfort in the familiar act of cleaning up the dishes.

"You're so adaptable. Sitting here, serving me refreshments as though you were in your own house." He finished his drink and leaned towards her, those penetrating brown eyes unwavering.

"Oh, but you must comprehend, it is because of my little customs that I am able to bear the strangeness of what has happened to me. We English have become proficient at recreating our society in whatever circumstances we find ourselves." Susannah finished collecting the dishes. "Chiang, what is this ship called?"

"This is the *Sheetlah*." He stood up. "And I have work to do. Thank you for the tea."

•　　　•　　　•

The next few days were full for Susannah, but gradually she found herself falling into a routine. She spent the morning and afternoon with Intlack and spent the evening doing what she wished, within the limits Chiang set for her. Usually this meant watching the multi-D programs. She kept intending to find the educational programs that Chiang said were available; but every night she found herself drawn into the continuing adventures of the willowy humanoid called Prull and his partially sentient vorpal, Pring.

Her relationship with Intlack was progressing rapidly, she felt. He very seldom showed her the hostility he had at first, and although he continued to bump into his pride once in a while, Susannah had no trouble finding ways around it.

The party was drawing rapidly nearer, and even isolated as she was, Susannah could feel the excitement on the ship. She was barely able to contain it herself. It seemed years since she had been to a party, and of course, she had never been to one like this. Chiang had not so far kept his promise about introducing her to other members of the ship's company, so she was looking forward to meeting them. And the party dress delivered by Yorty had her dancing around her room every evening as she tried it on in a variety of ways. Even the everyday dress seemed to her to be finer and more beautiful than anything she had owned on Earth.

Altogether, life seemed wonderful, and although loneliness for another human female sometimes struck her, it was a loneliness she was accustomed to. Even on Earth she had never had a close girlfriend. Her father's uncertain reputation combined with her mother's snobbishness had effectively barred her from associating too closely with either the high or the low of their society.

She tried to explain her longing to Intlack during one of their talks, but he couldn't grasp it.

[I hear what you are feeling. Why should you need someone else to know?]

Susannah tried not to laugh. "Intlack, you are not only an alien, you are a male alien. You may hear what I am feeling, but you cannot possibly understand it."

[That is true. For instance, just now you thought something about me — "self centered" I think it was. Of course I am self-centered. How else am I to be?]

"You can be self-aware without thinking of yourself as the center of everything." They were in the room with the view screen. The curtains were drawn at Susannah's request, but every once in a while, she peeked out in an effort to accustom herself to the infinite sight. Intlack's tentacles were weaving thoughtfully.

[I see only with my viewpoint, but there are other points to view?]

"Yes! And my point of view is very, very different from yours. But does that make it wrong?"

[Sometimes.]

This time she did laugh. "Intlack, you are incorrigible."

Intlack drew his head up.

[That is ... impossible to change? Then why are you trying to teach me?]

She sobered. "I am sorry. I shouldn't have said that. It was a sort of a joke. A poor joke."

[Joke?]

"Do you have jokes?"

[I do not think so. This is what makes you stretch your mouth?]

"Smile. Yes. Sometimes. Sometimes I smile just because I am happy. Jokes are a way of being happy with someone else. Sometimes jokes can make you happy when you are sad."

[Do you have another joke?]

"All my jokes are from my culture. They would not make sense to you."

Intlack shifted, and the lights struck sparks of color off the gems in his shell. Susannah admired the lovely and intricate patterns made by the jewels.

[This is part of what makes you lonely. No one to share your jokes with.]

"Yes! Intlack! You are seeing through my viewpoint!"

[It is difficult.]

"I know. I find it difficult to see through yours. Just as I find it difficult to look out through the screen here. It is so very different from what I am accustomed to."

[Different does not mean better — or worse?]

"No. Just — not the same. Sometimes it might be better or worse, sometimes it might be just — different."

[This is related to tolerance.]

"Yes! Seeing the points to view and accepting them."

[It takes time.]

"Oh, yes. I do not think it ever really ends. That is why you and I need to think before we communicate."

[You, too?]

"Do you not remember? You said yourself at the first dinner that I was not polite."

[True … Perhaps if I hear you being rude I could remind you to think!] He straightened up, pleased with himself.

"Why, that's a good idea, Intlack. And if I think you're about to — to be unwise — I could give you a signal — a secret signal."

[What is this — secret?]

"Well, something others don't know about." She smiled. "When I was young, my father would wink at me when he wanted me to meet him somewhere." She anticipated his question. "See my eye?" She demonstrated. "Then he would mention a place in conversation and when we could get free of other company, we would meet there! It was our secret."

[We could not have a secret signal. Anything you think, my parents would know.]

"Well, that's true. But we could have a secret from Chiang and the others on the ship. And maybe someday I'll learn to control my thoughts enough to hide them from your parents."

Intlack projected disbelief. *[You'll never have that much control. But it would be — smile-making — to have a secret from others. What could be our signal? I cannot wink.]*

"How about if we shake our heads. Like this?"

[Of course! Whenever I shake my head, you need to control yourself!]

"And you likewise!" Susannah laughed.

[This is a good plan.] Intlack practiced shaking his head. *[We can try it tonight at the gathering/meal/service.]*

"Tonight? Dinner is tonight?"

[Yes.]

"Then my trial time is up!" Susannah stood in dismay. She had expected to have more opportunities to charm Intlack.

[What is this 'charm'?]

Oh, dear. "Well, I — *mm* — I have been trying to be friendly with you, Intlack. To use my charm is to be friendly." She smiled.

[The echoes of your thoughts tell me charm/disarm/ captivate.] Intlack's tentacles were pointed straight at the ceiling. *[Using/wielding/manipulating — charm. This word connotes of diplomacy as you explained it to me. I think to be friendly and to be friends must not be the same thing. He moved forward. Do you wish me to be your friend.? Or do you wish me to be charmed? That would be helpful to your task here — for me to be charmed. Have you been friendly, because you had the friends feeling for me, or is this only diplomacy such as your mother used?]*

"Oh, no, Intlack! I truly wish to be friends — that is, I feel friendly to you —"

[I thought untruths could not be told with thoughts. But perhaps your species is capable of such. I must think on this.]

Intlack moved out the door.

"Intlack! Intlack!" She could hear Snotty lumbering down the corridor. Susannah grunted with frustration. She pulled the curtains and went back to her room.

When Chiang came in Susannah cried, "Why did you not tell me my time was up today!"

"Why? What have you done?"

"I have not done a thing! Why must you assume I have done something?"

"Experience."

"Well, I simply would have appreciated knowing that today was my last chance with Intlack before ..."

"Did you upset him somehow?"

"No! Well, perhaps a little. We simply spoke about charm, and I think he may have interpreted my remarks in the wrong manner. It is difficult to read the facial expressions of a snail."

"You don't say. However, he can read your thoughts."

"That is the problem. My thoughts are not always in the best of order."

"You don't say." He lay down on her bed and put his hands behind his head.

"Is that all you can say?"

"I could say that your thoughts probably express exactly what you feel, but you wouldn't like that."

"You mean — you are implying that I have been trying to charm him ..." Susannah sat down at her table.

"Is that what upset him? Well, haven't you? You want to stay on the *Sheetlah*, don't you?"

"Yes, but —"

"And you have known from the second day that you were on trial."

"Yes, but — oh, I was not so mercenary about it!"

"Why not?" Chiang stretched and sighed. "Susannah, you are the one who has confused Intlack about this. When you arrived, he would have expected nothing more from you than an attempt to do your job well enough to please his father — no matter what you had to do to succeed at that goal. From the Shill perspective, it is natural for you to use any means you can to achieve that. The Shill do not expect ethical considerations from barbarian species like ourselves. It is you who have taught Intlack that you have a different way of looking at it. He knows that in your culture, at least as you have explained it to him, there is such a thing as friendship for its own sake. You seem to have created a desire in him for something he has never had. A friend. Here's your tea."

"Oh, dear." Susannah watched the tea tray creature make its silent entrance. "Chiang, do the Shill have pets?"

"No. I don't think they would understand the concept. All their creatures have specific tasks. The Shill evolved by cooperating with the existing species on their planets and genetically engineering the workers they needed." He stretched and sat up.

"Pity. Intlack would benefit from having a pet to care for."

"Yeah, I can just see a dog trotting along after Snotty, yapping at his heels."

She made a face at him. "Not a dog! Something in a cage — like a rabbit. Do you want tea?" She began to pour out.

"Yeah, I think I would." He stood, stretched again, and took the two steps to the table. "Why don't you ever put this thing away? Never mind — I know. Because you never stop eating."

"Yes, and that reminds me. I need exercise."

He laughed. "I see the connection. Well, I'm not going to teach you *tai chi*. Talk to Dory, I'm sure she'll think of something." He drank his tea. "The Shill have no need of exercise. The rest of us have to find our own ways. Simtlack is usually helpful if given a specific request."

"You admire him, do you not? Simtlack. And you admire the Shill?"

"Why not? They're more intelligent and more advanced than any species on Earth or any other culture I've heard of. And they've done it without war. None."

She sipped her tea. "How can you say a species is more advanced when they are so mercenary? Using other species, but not assisting them to become more than they are. Not enlightening them."

He gave a bark of laughter. "Mercenary. You don't like that word. You think they should be enlightening the rest of the universe. Like the British empire, no doubt. Nobly assisting the ignorant masses to see all the material benefits of Empire while greedily helping themselves to all the resources those masses have been sitting on. Narrow minded, pompous and greedy. Those are the British I've seen. I warn you, Susannah. Don't try to enlighten creatures you don't understand. Stick to being mercenary."

"Do not worry," she snapped. "I do not anticipate being given the opportunity to do anything with these creatures. You can relax. I will not be present much longer to endanger you!"

Chiang stood up abruptly, spilling his tea. "You are the most self-centered creature I have ever met!" He stomped out.

"Bloody fool," muttered Susannah. "Calling *me* self-centered!" She cleaned up her dishes, put away her table, straightened her clothing, straightened her hair, looked around desperately for something else to do. Nothing. She turned on the multi-D, but for once Prull failed to interest her.

7

D ORY SENT FOR SUSANNAH because her new dress was ready. Susannah looked at it with a gasp of delight, but then wailed, "Oh, Dory! I do not think this lovely dress will help. They are not going to keep me! I have not charmed Intlack in any way! Why did you not tell me the next dinner is so soon? I upset Intlack by thinking about what you said. I just cannot seem to control my thoughts!"

[Oh, what a roasted old worm I am! I must teach you some things right away! You can't be going to that dinner unprotected! Relax your mind. Here, drink some tea. Think only of drinking tea. You trust me, don't you?]

"Yes, of course!" Susannah obediently drank her tea, wondering if her bladder would hold out.

Dory projected a sort of picture for her.

[There! Can you feel this?]

"What?"

[Can you feel anything? Around your thoughts?]

"Around my thoughts? Well, I — is it like — like a bit of sponge? A thin sponge around my thoughts? I can feel it, Dory."

[That's it! A mind shield. You have an unusually sensitive mind for your species.]

"What does it do?"

[It will hide anything but your surface thoughts from probing. Most of the time, only what you deliberately think at someone will be heard. With practice, it will become stronger, and you will be able to control the projection of your thoughts, as we telepaths do naturally. The more you practice feeling it, shaping, the stronger it will be and the more control you will have. You will also be able to protect any thought you wish from being read by almost any creature.]

"Even Simtlack?"

[Well, eventually, with enough practice. Simtlack is very strong. Is there something you want to keep from Simtlack?]

"No — just, you know — private feelings."

Dory chuckled. *[Of course. But let me tell you. Simtlack's probably not interested anyway.]*

Susannah sighed. "It all seems so complicated."

[Dory seemed surprised. Life is complicated, youngling. Don't you know that yet? Now the one who may be interested is Snactyl. She is the head of security. She's a snake, physically and mentally. Snactyl prefers to be able to read everyone.]

"Well, perhaps I should not then have a shield?"

[Boiling suns, everyone has a shield. You are perfectly within your rights. Yours may be a trifle stronger than some. I am very good at creating shields. It is just another form of spinning. You run along now. Have a bath and relax.]

Susannah went to the bathing chamber as ordered. "Anybody in there?" she called cautiously.

When she got no answer, she went in and fiddled with the buttons. She had had a bath before, but she had not yet mastered the controls. After getting several kinds of bubble bath and several scents, she managed to get the water running up into the softly padded tub. Such a magnificent improvement over a hip bath! I can never go back. She sank down luxuriously.

"Susannah! Excrement! Where are you?"

"Go 'way," mumbled Susannah, half asleep.

The door curtain swished aside. Susannah shrieked, and slid down under the bubbles, splashing water everywhere.

"Hey, watch it!" yelled Chiang.

"Remove yourself at once!"

"Ha! Outgrow this archaic modesty, why don't you? You're not on Earth!" Chiang leaned negligently against the doorframe.

"Out! Out! Out!"

"Such a temper! Where have you been this afternoon?"

"That is none of your concern."

"Everything you do is my concern."

"I will explain to Simtlack that I no longer need or desire a nursemaid. Now get out!"

He straightened up, his face dark with fury. "You do that. We'll see how long you last then!" He stalked out.

Susannah finished her bath quickly, relaxation gone. She returned to her room and put on her beautiful new dress, then sat down on her bed again to wait.

Was she self-centered? She was here because she had wanted adventure. She had certainly gotten what she wanted! But had she ever seriously considered what the Shill had wanted from her? Had she ever really been concerned about Intlack's needs?

Chiang knocked beside her door. "Ready?"

"Yes." She stepped out.

His eyes widened. "You look very — nice." He turned away and strode hastily along the corridor.

"Thank you," said Susannah. "Such high praise."

The dining room looked much the same as it had the first time. One difference Susannah noted was that Intlack's tentacles were not pointed in her direction. She got the impression that he was ignoring her. The second difference she noted was that there was no purple ziltlur on the table.

[Greetings, rumbled Simtlack. And welcome.]

"Thank you," said Susannah. She sank onto a pillow. She was more graceful than she had been the last time, because she had been practicing.

[Your time with us has been instructive for all, Susannah, came Cheetlon's soothing thought. Have you any impressions to share with us?]

Susannah groaned mentally, and hoped that the feeling was cloaked by her new shield.

What should she say? What would be diplomatic? She looked at Intlack, and decided against that. No diplomacy. She would tell them the truth. If she couldn't remain here on those terms, then … She couldn't think about the alternative. But what Chiang had said about Intlack … and about not attempting to enlighten these creatures … She had to admit that his perception about Intlack was probably correct. But if he thought she could remain without attempting to enlighten, then he didn't know Susannah Maureen Chambers McKay!

She took a deep breath and began: "I have enjoyed my time here immensely, Sir and Madame and Eldest. I hope that I have taught the Eldest a little about the culture of my birth. He has certainly taught me a great deal — both about Shill culture and about myself."

Intlack's tentacles finally swung around to her, but he projected no thoughts. Chiang was sitting quietly, watching her expressionlessly. Simtlack and Cheetlon were silent also, waiting. Susannah plunged on.

"I called Intlack 'self-centered' in one of our discussions recently, but Chiang advises me that the term describes me as well. I have concluded that he is correct. I came here with the arrogant presumption that I could easily teach an alien. I believe that I have taught him. But he has not always learned what I intended to teach. We have a saying on Earth, 'Practice what you preach.' I have not done that. I am sorry, Intlack. I would truly like to be your friend."

Intlack's tentacles remained steadily directed toward her, but for a long moment he was silent. Slowly, seeming puzzled, he thought, *[I hear what you say, but what you feel is very fuzzy. You are unclear. You have never been unclear before.]*

[Hmm?] Simtlack's attention sharpened. *[The Eldest is correct. You are attempting protection of your thoughts!]*

Susannah winced as the full force of Simtlack's thoughts centered on her.

[You have a mind shield! What is this? Chiang, what is this?]

"I know nothing about it, Sir! Susannah, galaxies preserve us! What have you done now?"

"Well, I — nothing much, I told Dory I was uncomfortable with the way my thoughts were so easily read and she helped me —"

"Helped you! You bloody little fool, shields are forbidden without the permission of the Diplomat! Why can't you —"

[Enough. This is ended. The Teacher 's trial period is over. She has offended again and will be left in the Alpha Centauri system. As per her contract, we will arrange for a trader to return her to Earth. Please depart.]

Susannah stood up. Chiang stood up. Chiang bowed, and Susannah imitated his motion. They turned to leave.

[Please wait. Father, please hear me.] Intlack's tentacles swiveled in distress. *[When the Teacher arrived, Mother pointed out to me that this is not her accustomed form of communication. I had forgotten that. I have listened to all her thoughts and feelings, and made no distinction between them. It is because of my discourtesy that she has felt the need for this shield. I listened to thoughts she did not intend to reveal, and I made judgments about the Teacher's character based on those private thoughts. Please do not dismiss her based on this transgression.]*

Susannah smiled at Intlack. "Thank you, my friend," she said.

Simtlack's projection was unyielding. *[Your statement does not change the circumstance of the forbidden being done.]*

"That is my fault," said Chiang. "I never fully explained to Susannah what was and was not forbidden. I did not want the responsibility of looking after her. I spent my time with her telling her that I did not want that duty, rather than in instructing her. I told her only to come to me before doing anything — which was clearly impossible for her, both because I am busy and because of the impulsive nature of her character."

[Father, Mother, please—]

[Hmm. Every creature wait.] Simtlack's tentacles were directed at Cheetlon.

Try as she might, Susannah could not receive a bit of their conversation. *I wonder if my shield will become that strong one day?* she thought. Then she remembered: *I must depart.* Desolation filled her at the thought. She opened her mouth to speak, then noticed Intlack. He was shaking his head with long swoops of his sinuous neck. Susannah closed her mouth and stared at him in astonishment. Then she remembered their signal. He was telling her not to interrupt his parents! She waited. She glanced at Chiang, but he did not seem to have noticed Intlack's odd behavior. Susannah sighed and shuffled her feet.

Simtlack and Cheetlon broke contact. Their tentacles swiveled to regard the rest of the party. Cheetlon's mellow tones thrummed in Susannah's head. She seemed amused.

[We have decided that the three of you need another trial period. Since you have all taken responsibility for each other, we will hold all of you responsible.]

Simtlack elaborated: *[Chiang, you must inform the Teacher fully of our law. Intlack, you must refrain from making communication difficult for the Teacher. Susannah-Teacher, you have until the next meal time to become Shillvilized. Simtlack straightened himself up. Make it so.]*

[But, Father — began Intlack.]

Susannah shook her head wildly.

[Excuse me, Father. You are wise.]

[The meal must begin. Chiang, Susannah, you may go.]

Susannah and Chiang went through the curtain. As they headed down the corridor, Susannah could hear Simtlack's intonation: *[We give thanks, Oh Master, for sustenance, life, color ...]*

Another trial period, thought Susannah. *Oh, well.* She would have to be circumspect in her teaching — for the time being. She glanced sideways at Chiang, knowing he must be seething. He controlled himself until they reached her room.

"When —"

"I know, I know. When will I learn — this is a strange culture, and I don't know what is going on. I should ask you first before doing such crazy things as trying to protect my thoughts from strangers poking around in them ..." Susannah smiled at his furious face.

Chiang stuttered, "You are — you cannot — I will never — "He gave up and stomped out of the room.

Susannah thought that it was too bad he didn't have a door to slam. She supposed she should not have been so flippant, but really! All's well that ends well, she should have told him. No harm done. And she would be more careful — for the time being. At least until after the party.

The party! Susannah smiled. A new dress and a party to go to. how could Chiang expect her to think seriously with such a prospect ahead of her? She could hardly wait for that party ...

8

W HEN SUSANNAH WALKED into the party that night, she did not see every eye turn to her, but she did see a few. Her blue dress shimmered, and its silvery highlights sparkled. One of her arms was bare, and one side of the dress was slit to the knee! Susannah had protested, but Dory had insisted.

Actually, Aunt Dory had wanted to slit it to her thigh, but Susannah had refused to wear it if she did. Susannah told Dory that she came from a culture that could not even say the word "leg," let alone show one. Dory had not believed her. Susannah's hair was looped on one side with silver ribbons and left hanging to her waist in the back, and she wore soft, comfortable silver shoes. Better for dancing, Dory had said. Susannah had approved the footwear change wholeheartedly.

Her first look around reminded her of a forest. Apparently a snail's idea of beautiful decorations were trees, vines and bushes, with what appeared to Susannah to be a small swamp on one side of the room. Looking at the scene with fascination, Susannah realized that she could not always tell the sentient beings from the furniture and decorations. There was a tall form which she had taken to be a tree, until she noticed another creature speaking to it. The whole room had a pungent smell which Susannah associated with loamy earth and swamp grass, mixed with the sweat and scents of partying creatures.

[Well,] Dory chuckled from behind her. *[I think you've tickled their tentacles.]*

Susannah laughed and looked around at the seamstress who sat in her wheelchair, pushed by Yorty. Dory had told Susannah that she could still walk but preferred to ride, because old segments strain easily. Dory was wearing a silk sheath which rippled with iridescent color; over her lap was a brilliantly blue shawl rather than the afghan.

[Push me over near a table,] Dory ordered Yorty, then looked around in annoyance as he spoke. He spoke too quickly for Susannah's translator to catch his words. *[I know I could run it with my thoughts, but I prefer to think about other things. I've told you that since you were a tadpole. Now push me over there, or I'll tell Snactyl about your snake skin belt.]* She was immediately raced to a table. *[All right, go!]*

Yorty scuttled over to a refreshment table, where he collected four drinks and two plates of food.

"Would you like a drink, Dory?"

[No thank you, my dear. You mingle a bit. But remember what I told you.]

Susannah took one step away, immediately feeling horribly vulnerable. She took a deep breath and kept going. Strange creatures were making strange noises and eating strange foods everywhere. On one table she saw what appeared to be ziltlur. She shuddered and turned away.

She felt someone touching the hair hanging down her back. She jumped away from the sensation and turned around. A being she tentatively identified as a very large beaver faced her, fingered paw still outstretched.

"I like your fur!" The scratchy voice was accurately duplicated by the translator. His head just reached her shoulder, and he was dressed in a uniform of pink and green with gold piping. A cap with a feather was set at an angle between his small ears.

"Well, thank you," said Susannah, blinking. All the party protocol her mother had so carefully imbued her with was going to prove useless here, she could see.

"May I be knowing your name?"

"I'm Susannah — Teacher."

"Yes, I know. I be the Captain, so I know all aboard."

The Captain! Susannah was relieved that she had not slapped his paw away as had been her first instinct.

"I ask so as to have permission to be using your name, you see,"

"Oh! Yes, please do, Captain."

"My name be Julian. Please to use it?"

"Of course, Julian."

"The seamstress created supremely for you."

"Oh, yes, she did. I have never been attired so well." She relaxed a bit. This was simply party small talk, after all.

"Would you be enjoying your living on the *Sheetlah*?"

"Yes, I be — I am, but naturally it is quite different from what I am accustomed to."

"Ah, yes, Earth. Many say Earth be of no contribution to the Universe, but if lovely female members with lovely fur grow there — can't be all bad." His ears twitched.

Susannah smiled. This sort of talk she was entirely accustomed to. "Oh, but Captain, you must have encountered many females in your travels on this beautiful ship. Tell me about the *Sheetlah*. You must be so very clever to sail her through space as you do."

The beaver slapped his tail against the floor and was off, detailing for her the intricacies of his ship. Susannah thought complacently that she had never met a captain yet who could resist talking about his ship — whether he considered her a tub or the finest vessel in existence. Julian was obviously one of the latter.

"Julian, you are a fine Captain, but your sself-proclaimed reputation ass an entransser iss obviousssly undesserved."

Susannah shrank away from the enormous snake who had glided silently up to them. The snake was almost lost in the swirl of color around her; she wore nothing but her own green, black and dark red skin.

The beaver lost his happy glow and glared up at the snake. "Just because you be interested in nothing but yourself, fine Snactyl, and been entranced never, be not meaning that other, more cultured females cannot be appreciating good conversation about *Sheetlah*!"

"I have heard that Earth creaturess are weak-minded, but I find it hard to believe they are sso vacuum-headed ass that."

Susannah gathered all her determination and looked the huge snake in the eye. "I was enjoying the Captain's talk. I —" She forgot what she was saying. The snake's eyes were large, as large as her fist, and the pupils were widening slits of yellow ...

The Captain stepped between them and waved a paw.

"Be not pulling thy serpent tricks on this newcome female, Snactyl. Be showing some decency. This be a party."

The snake pulled her head back as Susannah drew a shaky breath. "You are ssuch an excssitable fellow, Captain. I was not doing her harm. Wass I, Ssussanah? You will learn, if you sstay with uss long, that our Captain makess novass out of dead ssuns. It iss what hass kept the *Sheetlah* ssafe through many passages." The snake lowered her head to the Captain's level. "Issn't that right, Ssir?" The beaver glared at her, and she laughed with a soft hissing. "It hass been good to meet you, Earthwoman. I have neglected you, and I am ssorry for thiss. The vissiting ambassadorss have been a disstraction. I will csertainly make an effort to know you better sson. That iss a promissse." She glided away.

Susannah shivered.

"Please," said the Captain. "Be not troubled by Snactyl. She behaves so to all. It is her nature and her obligation." He touched Susannah's hair gently. "What can one be expecting from a furless creature?" She had to laugh at that, and the Captain slapped his tail gently. "Allow me to give your name to shipmates of more agreeable natures?"

"I would be delighted." She took the arm he offered, although he had to reach up, and she down, for him to do so. His fur was soft and warm, and she could feel the hard muscle underneath.

As they strolled, she looked around her at the other creatures. She saw a lizard-like creature walking on its hind legs. It wore a lot of ribbons wrapped around its scaly red body. She saw a sort of bear with a long, fluffy tail. It walked on all fours and swung the tail from side to side. It wore a stiff, shiny armor which rippled as it walked. Then she saw a humanoid who was definitely female. Susannah gasped with a mixture of pleasure and shock. The woman was very beautiful, with bronze skin and black hair wrapped around her neck like a collar. Susannah was delighted to see a female so like herself, but astounded to see that the woman wore a long skirt of brilliant scarlet — but no blouse or top, simply a broad, shiny gold band around her breasts. Susannah stared.

"You see Cayannah," noted the Captain, and steered her in that direction.

"Cayannah," breathed Susannah. "Does she live on the *Sheetlah*?"

"No, Cayannah be Amusant. Amusant be traveling entertainers, ship drifters. Amusant be always welcome everywhere."

"I can see why," murmured Susannah.

"Be keeping the new female to thyself, Sir? Or be giving some of these work drowned underlings a chance for speech with beautiful furred creature?" Two more beavers in the scarlet and green uniforms were facing them. Neither had a feather in his cap.

"Teacher be not needing to learn from scruffy specimens like thee." The Captain paused. "But as you be in our way ... Susannah, these be Navigator Ashley and First Officer Bastion. Ashley be the quiet one."

Ashley smiled. Bastion smoothly elbowed him aside and took her other arm. "Our Captain been boring you with full specifications on *Sheetlah*?"

"No, indeed, he was not boring me."

Bastion laughed knowingly. "I tell you, he be in love with *Sheetlah* — no time for other females."

"Ahh," said the Captain, "so I suppose she be better off with a spewing torrent of words like you?"

"Not so! I be going to tell her to behold Ashley, finely furred and scarce a ripple of speech from him!"

Ashley's ears twitched as Susannah glanced at him with a smile. His hat slid forward over one brown eye. His shipmates laughed at him as he adjusted it.

"Be very dashing, Ashley!" laughed Bastion.

"I be introducing Susannah to Cayannah," said the Captain.

"Ahh!" said Bastion happily. He released her arm and spurted ahead to gain the Amusant's attention.

The Captain chuckled.

Ashley quietly took her arm. "The only thing to distract Bastion from one beautiful female be another," he said mildly.

The Captain laughed, his tail slapping. "You should be saying such when Bastion be near, he be not calling you a ripple then."

Ashley smiled. They drew near to the group surrounding Cayannah. Bastion had squirmed through the crowd and was edging the competition out with practiced elbows. In a moment he had turned Cayannah to face them. "Cayannah-Amusant," he said formally, "Susannah-Teacher."

The bronze woman smiled. Bells on her wrists tinkled as she put out her hand. "It is so wonderful to meet a humanoid female!" Gray eyes met golden brown and white hand met bronze.

She makes it seem as though I am the only one in the world for her at this moment! "I am delighted to meet you."

"We must be friends," said Cayannah. "Females without fur or scales must stick together." She shed her smile around the group then, like a queen scattering gold coins.

"There be no need for sticking together," said the Captain. "We be only agreeable to lovely female creatures."

"Yes," said Bastion. "But if it be sticking you wish, I be gladsome to participate!"

Susannah looked at his furry face doubtfully.

Cayannah laughed and said, "All know that beavers prefer to be horizontal, but most particularly Bastion of the *Sheetlah*!"

Susannah swallowed. She would have to be very cautious in her flirting with these fellows!

Ashley said softly, "Comes of being born in wealthy family. Never working, Bastion, always be floating on the Ripplefree with refreshments on his belly."

Bastion smiled, showing all his teeth. "Teeth be as sharp as thine, Ashley. Be wanting a log to test?"

"I do not think that is necessary," said Cayannah soothingly. "We can see what fine teeth you have. Can we not, Susannah?"

"Oh, yes indeed! All three of you!"

Susannah was startled by a tap on her shoulder. She looked around to see Yorty simultaneously tapping on her shoulder and Cayannah's, eating what appeared to be a pastry and filling a glass form a bottle. Her translator reported that he said, "Severance is necessitated. Untranslatable."

"Pardon me?" said Susannah.

Cayannah laughed her musical laugh and said, "If you want people to understand you, Yortling, don't talk with your mouth full. Did you say Aunt Dory wants to see us? Very well." She linked her arm with Susannah's and led her away from the disappointed beavers. "A walk across the room can be theater, can't it, Susannah. You and I, we will be the stars tonight!"

"Oh, no Cayannah. It is you they watch. Most oft when I attempt a graceful sashay across the room, I stumble and fall!"

"That merely shows how well you know they are looking, but you have not yet accepted their admiration. It is your Creator who is truly being complimented, think of that." Cayannah made a sweeping gesture toward Susannah's form, her bracelets tinkling. "It is your seamstress' due, and your hairdresser's, your body painter's and whomever else has assisted you in appearing as you appear this night. Many people have labored for you. Receive with grace on their behalf."

[Well, I see you two have made a pair. I wish I could take credit for both of you!]

Cayannah winked at Susannah.

[Cayannnah, who spun your skirt? Streelbad? I might have known. That spider clothes humanoids so well. I told you, Susannah, to leave your mammary glands more exposed. Males of all vertebrate species are attracted to mammary glands. It's one of the great mysteries of the galaxy.]

Susannah fumbled for words. "It is — not the custom — where I come from. At any rate, not to such an extent."

Cayannah nodded. "The customs of childhood are hard to outgrow. And sometimes, they should not be. Her dress is lovely as it is, Dory." She half closed her dark eyes. "Sometimes the wonderment about what is hidden is more intriguing."

Dory rocked gently in her chair. *[Yes, yes. So true.]* She enjoyed her satisfaction for a moment, then became serious. *[Susannah, did I see Snactyl speaking with you?]*

Susannah met the old worm's eyes with reawakened anxiety. "Yes, and I don't think she —"

[Oh, that is well.] Dory explained smugly: *[Cayannah, I gave Susannah a mind shield. Snactyl did not detect it. She will certainly not approve.]* She gave out the low hiss which Susannah had come to realize was her laughter.

"Every warm-blooded female needs a mind shield. Snactyl does not understand that and never will."

[Exactly.]

"No one would dare try to read Snactyl's thoughts —except Simtlack. And the only secrets she can comprehend are political ones. Where is the Family, Dory?"

[They are with the ambassadors, Screel One and Screel Two. I have never learned to appreciate Creels. They all sound alike to me.]

"They do not appreciate Amusants." It was obvious that was enough for Cayannah to dismiss them.

"What are they?" Susannah looked around at the multitude of creatures, wondering what sort the experienced Cayannah and Dory could agree against.

[They are creatures of a swamp world. One mind, many colonies of drudging workers, interested only in their own murky selves. The ambassadors are from the colony whose turn it is to handle stellar politics, and the pair whose turn it happens to be to go off planet.]

"That's the theory," said Cayannah. "Since no one can tell them apart, it may be there are only these two, and they just change their names! Have you heard that one?"

Dory hissed with laughter. *[Yes, but Simtlack says he can tell them apart.]*

"Perhaps that is why he has been more successful parleying with them than anyone else." Cayannah turned to Susannah. "They have a solar system full of resources the rest of the quadrant would like to exploit. Some of the less scrupulous species have been making inroads without the Creels' consent, since they seemed to be no threat and to care for nothing but their swamp. Lately, however, they have become annoyed. It seems to be a religious thing, as near as I can tell. They worship their sky view and do not want it cluttered with alien installations." Cayannah shrugged. "They have appealed to the Family for assistance in controlling the scavengers. Several times treaties have been proposed, but the Creels have no needs; they do not wear clothing, do not drink anything but their own swamp water, or eat anything but their own swamp plants. There is nothing to be traded with them. All they want is protection, so Simtlack has been trying to find a way to bargain with that, and still find a way to use their resources." She looked thoughtful. "Perhaps the reason Simtlack has been so successful is because the Families also have few vices and are very religious."

Dory nodded her upper segments. *[It's their belief system. Their Creator requires them to be moderate in all things. She hissed happily. Thank the Stars my belief system holds a more liberal Creator!]*

"Simtlack's prayer the night I had dinner with them was beautiful," murmured Susannah.

It had surprised her that a creature so alien could have such lofty thoughts. Her mother had been staunchly Church of England, but there had never seemed to Susannah to be much depth to her belief. The activity of being religious seemed to entail attending services, collecting clothing for the much-discussed but never seen poor, and serving tea to the minister's wife. Her father had scoffed at any and all religious beliefs, and at the death of her mother, Susannah had ceased her vaguely religious practices without regret. It was astounding to come to such an exotic place so far from home and find there creatures which actually lived out their beliefs. Susannah filed the puzzle away for future consideration.

"And Shill meals are far more impressive on their home world," Cayannah was saying.

[Have you been there?] Dory sounded surprised.]

"Yes, but I didn't enjoy it."

Dory nodded, hissing. *[No male vertebrates!]*

Cayannah laughed. "Your swift understanding reveals your own mind, Aunt Dory!"

[I don't deny it! I don't deny it! But these segments strain too easily now. That is all behind me.]

"Of course it is!" Cayannah put one tinkling hand on Dory's chair arm. "Worms always twine from behind!"

Susannah stared at the laughing creatures and tried not to show her shock.

[Poor Susannah, we have outraged her sensibilities again. Of all the species I have come across, I think Earth creatures are the most prudish at the outset, and the quickest to adapt in time.]

Cayannah nodded, still laughing. "Your theory may not hold up this time, though. Susannah does not look as though she will adapt. And you really have very few Earth folk to judge by, since they have not yet achieved interstellar travel."

[True, true.]

A furry nose poked around Dory's chair. "You have monopolized the females long enough, old wormy one. Be time for dancing!"

9

S USANNAH LOOKED DOWN at the beavers. There were only two, neither with a feather in his cap. "Captain be called to work," said Ashley, holding up his arm to Cayannah. "So sad."

"Yes, be very dry for Captain," said Bastion, holding his furry arm out to Susannah.

"Oh, but I don't know —" Susannah was suddenly aware of how strange the music was — and how strange her partner was.

"Be not needing to know," said Bastion, "be only needing to feel. He swept her onto the floor. The music was a swirl of pleasant sounds, but no discernible (to Susannah) beat. Bastion's movements seemed to have no pattern. "Be trying too hard," he said, swinging her around. "Must relax." His muscular agility seemed to compensate for the fact that his partner was a foot taller than he.

Susannah tried to relax, and was just beginning to to think she had found a rhythm when the music died away with a moan.

"What's wrong?"

"Be nothing wrong. Be rest. Not tired?"

"Oh, no. Be just getting accustomed to it!"

He grinned and his incisors gleamed. "Be thirsty?"

"Yes!"

"Be right back." He zipped away through the crowd.

Susannah leaned against a tree and watched the other creatures getting refreshments. She saw beings crawling, flying, slithering, and walking. She saw scales, feathers, skin of all colors and — metal?

As she craned her neck to get a better view, the figure was gone. She estimated there were about one hundred creatures present. She wondered how many were normally on the *Sheetlah* and how many were aboard for the occasion. She wondered how long Cayannah would be aboard. She would have to ask Bastion. When he zipped back to her side, he was holding a tall, green glass.

"Not ziltlur — or anything like it?"

"No, no, ziltlur make dancing too difficult."

She laughed. "Undoubtedly. Thank you." She sipped. "Ooh. Fizzy! Bastion, how many people — that is, how many are usually aboard the *Sheetlah*?"

"Changes muchly." Bastion sipped his own drink and carefully wiped the fur over his mouth with his paw. "Crew be only forty, but Simtlack be having visitors often. *Sheetlah* able to hold two hundred easily. Time was we evacuated sick city of four hundred. Not easy." He shook his head.

"What do you mean, sick city?"

He frowned. "Foreign pirate land without permission, bring bad disease. City contaminated. We rescue and quarantine survivors, take to medical base." He grinned fearsomely. "Then we return and get that pirate good, by my incisors!"

"Oh." Susannah eyed him doubtfully, and decided not to ask for details.

Bastion held out his paw. "Music be starting again."

She finished her drink and set it down on what appeared to be a tree stump. Bastion's paw felt warm and soft. The dance was easier for her to feel this time. Bastion's guidance was sure and exhilarating. His teeth flashed as the music ended, and he put his arm around her. Susannah felt a moment's panic, then felt herself pulled free.

"Be time for more experienced partner, Bastion."

"Bah! Can't be meaning you! Lose your partner, Lumberjoint?"

"Captain," admitted Ashley. He held out his paw as Susannah turned to Bastion.

"Thank you. You were a wonderful teacher!"

After dancing with Ashley, she danced with the Captain, and after the Captain with a lizard-like creature (who made her nervous by slipping his tongue in and out as he spoke), and after that a humanoid with purple eyes and a tail. After that she lost track. A few of her partners got her more refreshments, and one of them, fortunately, was able to direct her when she asked for humanoid waste management facilities. When she had relieved herself, she danced with him again. When the music drew to a close, he shook his mane and told her she was a fine dancer and a fine looking female, and it would be fine to dance with her again later. If she ever needed a warrior, he was a fine one and would be delighted to oblige.

"I would be pleased to dance again now," said Susannah boldly. She felt rather lightheaded, and she wondered if one of her partners might have served her something a bit potent.

"Now? Now is time for the Dalven!" said the lion and trotted off.

Susannah had to laugh, because he reminded her so much of a Colonel she had met once. But who or what was the Dalven? She looked around for a familiar face, but discovered she was on the far side of the swamp from Dory, and she saw no one she knew nearby — except Snactyl. The sight of the enormous snake caused the sweat to grow cold on her brow. She took a step backward, and felt water soaking her foot. She looked down with astonishment; she had stepped into the swamp.

"Oh, bloody luck!' she muttered, but Snactyl was still in sight, so mincingly she stepped further into the swamp in order to hide behind a tree. She lifted her skirt out of danger and peeked around the tree, leaning against it for support. Snactyl was still there, her red-scaled head swinging back and forth as she moved slowly in Susannah's direction.

She's looking for me! Susannah glanced behind her. The wall. She could creep along the wall through the swamp, or step out in the open. Without hesitation, she hitched her dress higher and squelched along the wall.

When she caught the tickle of voices in her head, she was relieved. She must be nearing the edge of the swamp! The next instant she spotted a clearing and stopped short, just out of sight of the creatures gathered there. It was the Creel ambassadors and the Family. The Creels were short, grayish blobs with no feet and arms. They seemed to simply ooze in and out. They were speaking simultaneously. Fascinated by the way their bodies constantly changed, like clay on a potter's wheel, Susannah leaned forward.

[We ask only this, the simultaneous voices were saying, that you pledge to us the accounts of Shill duplicity that we have heard are untrue. We are told the pirate attacks were arranged by your agents. May the sun shine on you for a thousand days if this is so.]

[Not so, asserted Simtlack.] His outrage was painful to Susannah's head. *[The Shill are not duplicitous. By the Shell, I pledge this to you.]*

Intlack's thoughts gave a wordless surge of support to his father's. Knowing how proud he was, Susannah could well imagine how the Creels' charge must hurt him.

[You understand we cannot stop the encroaching which alters our prayers. If the stars cannot be as we need them when the mist clears in the sun's second cycle ...] The Creels' arms met and merged. *[We will withdraw to our pits and await the end of your empire.]*

Some threat, thought Susannah. *I should think Simtlack would be delighted to see the last of your muddy hides.*

[What thought was that?] The Creels separated their arms. *[This gladdens you, Shill Simtlack?]*

[No!] Simtlack's bellow was deafening.

Susannah turned to run. She took a step forward, and disaster clutched her in its arms once again. Her shoe hit a patch of mud, her arms flailed wildly, and she went down with a cry and a splash, brackish water splattering as far as the Family, where they watched, appalled. Exclamations echoed in her head, with Intlack's excited outburst overall: *[It is the Teacher, Father. She has been spying!]*

Susannah tried never to remember her humiliating exit from the swamp, propelled by Simtlack's iron grip on her mind. Simtlack's thought/bellow for Snactyl brought the party to a halt. Snactyl's approach sent Susannah into a panic, and the shocked faces of her new friends made her blush. Dory's voice in her brain demanded the story swiftly, but Simtlack's outraged blast caused the old worm to shrink in her chair, and Snactyl's eyes on Susannah's drove all independent thought from her head.

When awareness returned to her, she felt her brain had been wrung out like a dishrag, and her beautiful dress, stiff with dried swamp water, made her feel as used. She pushed herself up off the cushion on the floor — no comforting rumble or soft feathers here — and looked around with a wince at the gray room. Gray! She hung her head and tried not to wonder what was going to be done with her.

What seemed a very long time later, the door (a real door) opened to admit a creature like Yorty. She wasn't sure if it was Yorty or another of his species. He made no sound, merely dumped two trays on the floor and bolted before she could even open her mouth. Her many questions tasted so bitter, trapped in her mouth, that she could not eat. After a long, bored interval, she did poke at the food for something to do. There was a paper underneath the greens.

"Susannah," she read, "thoughts being monitored, so I write. Your friends trying, but Simtlack won't speak while Creels still here. Don't despair. Dory."

Susannah felt tears come to her eyes. She wasn't forgotten. But who, exactly, were her friends, and what were they trying to do? Had Chiang helped Dory with the note, or was there someone else who could write English? Where had Chiang been all this time, anyway? She chewed listlessly on a vegetable stick.

It was all so confusing and frightening. What was the penalty for spying here? She remembered Chiang's warnings when she had first arrived. If only she had paid more attention to him!

When Snactyl entered the room at last, Susannah felt almost glad to face her. After all, she was innocent! It was all a silly misunderstanding. Surely Snactyl would be able to "hear" that. But her hope dissipated with Snactyl's first hiss.

"Ssusannah-Teacher. You have done a desspicable thing. Ssimtlack iss so angry he refusses to ssee you. What have you to ssay?"

Susannah stood up, trying to rebuild her nerve and avoid those slitted eyes. "I am not a spy! I want to see Simtlack!"

"Ass I ssaid, Ssimtlack will not condesscend to ssee you!"

"Then allow me to see Cheetlon!"

"The Firsst Conssort hass better thingss to do." Snactyl wove slowly back and forth, her gleaming eyes fixed on Susannah, who carefully avoided meeting them. The musty smell of the snake was gradually filling the small room, making Susannah gasp for breath.

"Chiang? Where is he? He wasn't at the party."

"No, he wassn't. Wass he suppossed to be? Iss he your contact? Iss that why you got caught, becausse he wass not there to assist you?" Snactyl lowered her head and pushed closer to Susannah.

"No! No, of course not!" Susannah's eyes snapped up and she was lost ...

The headache was fierce.

Susannah writhed on her pallet, trying to avoid consciousness, without knowing why she dreaded it. But then she was conscious, and she remembered. She lay on the floor, clutching the pillow, too depressed to do anything else.

When she heard a noise at the door, she was terrified, and then horrified by her terror. What had happened to her? What had Snactyl done that it had turned her into a gibbering coward? But if the snake tried it again, she knew she would scream, shriek at the top of her lungs — she opened her mouth —

"Shh! By the Buddha!" Chiang threw himself to his knees at her side and clamped a hand over her mouth. "What's gotten into you? I didn't think it was possible for things to be worse, but you may manage it yet. Are you all right?" He pulled his hand away from her face.

She looked up at him with wild eyes. "What the bloody heck are you doing? Where have you been? Why were you not at the party when I needed you?"

He sat up abruptly, saying in a high sarcastic voice, "Oh thank you, Chiang, for taking the risk of coming to see me! I was so worried about you when you didn't show up at the party! I was sure you wouldn't miss it on purpose! I am so glad to see you in good health!" He stood up. "I don't know why I came here to help you, you ungrateful bucket of worm puke!" He headed for the door.

"Do not leave me!" Susannah knelt and made grab at his legs. "Oh, Chiang, I am sorry! Please, please do not go!"

"That's more like it. Do you promise to be quiet and listen?" She nodded. "You're in a mess." She nodded again. "I may be able to get you out of it." She opened her mouth. "Quiet! You've been charged with the Shill variety of treason. It's an unreasonable charge, given that you are not a member of the crew and nothing in your contract said anything about you being loyal to the Shill or their allies. I know you didn't read your contract, but I did. The biggest problem right now is Snactyl's antagonism. I don't know what you did to anger her, but — Don't talk! — but the first thing we have to do is placate her. Since she happens to be a friend of mine, I may be able to help you there. The second thing we have to do is get Simtlack to see you. Right now he refuses to say anything about you, and he could leave it that way indefinitely." Susannah moaned. "I think he's been waiting for the Creels to leave. Unfortunately, they seem to have decided you're a test case to see whether the Shill are serious in their commitment to Creel interests." He shook out his robes and crouched down next to her. "Now what I want you to do is tell me exactly what happened at the party." He folded his arms. "All right, talk."

"Oh, Chiang, Snactyl is not your friend, she accused you of being my contact and —"

"Stop. The party."

"But you did not hear what I —" Chiang stood and turned toward the door. "All right! All right! The party! At the party, it was just an error, I was frightened of Snactyl from the first minute I met her —"

"When was that? What happened?"

Susannah went through the whole story as completely as she could. She described dancing with the beavers and explained how the Captain had vanquished Snactyl for her.

"Ahh! So you didn't anger her, that wooden-headed beaver did!"

"That beaver was protecting me from your good friend's assault on my mind!"

"That beaver has a long standing feud with Snactyl which provides him with a good deal of amusement. But he is the Captain, of proven ability and loyalty, and it makes no difference if he annoys her. You have no status here, as I have told you time and again, and you cannot afford to antagonize, of all creatures, the one whose responsibility is the security of this ship!" His voice lowered to a mutter. "Those beavers think all they have to do is show their teeth to have every female falling into their furry arms." His voice rose angrily. "You may be susceptible, but Snactyl is not, and they can't forgive her that! She wasn't assaulting you, she was just getting to know you … Her technique is just a little crude."

"Crude! Crude! Crude like a cabin boy trying to be butler to the queen! It felt like my head was coming apart!"

"Which might not be a bad thing! Oh, tell me about the rest of the party." He sat down on her pillow with a disgusted grunt.

Frowning back at him, Susannah squatted on the floor and told him about her attempt to avoid Snactyl which had caused her to enter the swamp.

"So that is all you heard?" he asked when she was done.

"That is all."

"Not much there that everyone doesn't know, anyway."

"Why does Snactyl not know I am not a spy? If she is such a great mind reader?"

"She can't get through your bloody mind shield, that's why! That stupid old worm made it so strong even Snactyl can't get through it. If it weren't for that interfering seamstress, you wouldn't be in all this trouble."

"Dory said it would be all right ..."

"Dory and Snactyl hate each other. That old worm grew up before the Universal Council! Her species and Snactyl's are old rivals. Why can't you get it through your skull that you know next to nothing about the society you're living in?"

"Why have you not been more thorough in teaching me? Whose fault is it if I do not understand what you think I ought to know? Dory has at least been teaching me what she thinks I ought to know!"

"I told you I was bound to fail at this job!"

"Well, is that not so very convenient for you! A self-fulfilling prophecy! Congratulations! Please do not allow yourself to feel any responsibility on my account." Susannah tossed her head back, and the last of the piled curls piled fell over her eyes. She thrust them back, suppressing angry tears. "I chose to come here, and I am responsible for what has happened to me, no one else!"

He was silent, his brown eyes unreadable. "Good," he said finally. He stood and walked to the door. "Although I am sorry," he said without looking at her.

"Oh, sod it!" she said violently as the door shut behind him. "Sod it! Bloody hell!" She swore the few swear words she knew over again. She would not cry. She would not cry!

1.0

T IME PASSED. At first, she wished she knew how much time was
passing. Then she realized she didn't care. Time just passed —
or perhaps it didn't. She stopped thinking about it one or the other.
She used the waste facilities in the wall. She munched on limp
greens and drank tea. She slept on her pallet, clutching the pillow.
Sometimes the tea and the greens were changed by the silent Yorty
lookalike, but they did not speak to each other. She sank into a deep
hole within herself where her regrets did not torture her.

Eventually she had a visitor. He crawled in slowly as Snotty
held the door for him. Susannah looked up, blinking slowly. Her
metabolism seemed to have slowed — her breath came deep and
shallow. She looked at Intlack, but felt no impulse to speak to him.

[So, he thought at her eventually, it is true.]

Susannah did not even wonder what he meant. She looked
at him, watching his tentacles swiveling slowly around.

*[You are a mess. I investigated reports of humans
imprisoned. I learned that humans are so social that most cannot
survive solitary confinement. You appear to be failing.]*

Failing? Susannah wondered about that. Had she not already failed? "I already

failed," she tried to say, but her voice was squeaky.

Intlack, however, caught the thought. *[Failing? Growing ill/declining/decaying?]*

Susannah tried to think. Communication seemed such a great deal of work. "Failing," she muttered. "Failing ... unsuccessful, at fault, fruitless, useless, worthless ..." She closed her eyes. She wanted to sleep.

Intlack slammed against her brain with almost as much force as his father might have used — or at least, so it seemed to Susannah. *[Teacher!]*

She jerked her head up. "What?" She put her hands to her head. "Oh, Intlack, do

not do that!"

[Communicate. The Creels want you killed. I come to assist you. Tell me all that occurred at the party.]

"Oh, that would take so long ..."

[You have time. I am willing to take time. Do you disdain my efforts?]

That cut through her despair. "Disdain? Intlack, how could I disdain anything about you?"

[Exactly. So, explain to me the party.]

Susannah sighed. "All right." She did as she had with Chiang, began at the beginning and attempted to take him through the whole evening.

[So, you did hear some of what we discussed. That is unfortunate. And you show me this clumsy fall, and your fear of Snactyl, but I find it difficult to contemplate. Perhaps you have learned more about disguising your thoughts than you say.]

"Oh, no, Intlack! You must believe me! I am not disguising anything. Snactyl's probing was like an axe slashing into my brain!"

[I do not know this axe, but I believe you mean that Snactyl has no delicacy.]

"Delicacy!" Susannah snorted, sitting up straighter. "She has all the delicacy of an inebriated dock worker! And you know how clumsy I am! I tripped and fell on the dinner table the first night we met!

[*What is this?*]

"I tripped — Oh!" Susannah stopped, hand to her mouth.

[*Explain.*]

"I — cannot."

[*You are hiding something.*]

"No. Yes — Chiang told me to."

[*So — Chiang is your accomplice!*]

"No! *No!* I cannot tell you of it because Chiang said your father declared it a nihilism!"

Intlack broadcast outrage. [*You know it is forbidden to speak of a nihilism. Are you trying to make things worse?*]

"Of course not! Why in God's name would I do that? But you demanded — Oh, Intlack, I don't think I can get into more trouble than I am in already!"

[*Perhaps not. But if you spoke of this to my father it would be very, very painful for you.*]

He slithered a few inches across the floor. His version of pacing, Susannah believed. She ventured to suggest something. "Your father does not know me as well as you do, I think. I just wanted to give an example of how clumsy I can be when I am — when I have had spirits to drink."

Intlack slithered a little more. [*Very well,*] he said at last.

Susannah wondered if it was his sense of justice or plain curiosity which led him to do it. But he remained still as she pictured for him the first dinner when she had landed full length on the table.

[*My father is strong. He would not have allowed you to think of this. Perhaps it will be better if you die. You confuse me. I should not be confused.*] He slithered toward the door.

Susannah sucked in her breath. "Intlack, everyone gets confused sometimes!"

[*Not my father. Not my mother.*]

"Well ... They are adults. You are young and growing and learning new things. Please, Intlack ... Is that a reason to let me die?"

[Your life is more important to you than it is to me. Although I will regret its end.]

"Intlack, there is another point to view! Tell me you will think on it!"

The door opened and Intlack slithered out. He did not respond to her plea.

Susannah threw back her head. "I will not cry."

Time crawled. Like a snail. Like a slimy, slithery, slick-minded snail. She tried to regain the thoughtlessness she had had, but it was gone. Thoughts came. And regrets. She could only endure them.

Chiang had been right all along. She knew nothing about this society. She did not know what feuds there were between species. Why had she not thought that there would be feuds? Goodness knew there were enough in her own world. She did not even know what the Universal Council was, let alone its laws. She did not know the protocol here. How many times had her father told her to always be sure she understood the etiquette of any group she found herself in? Her mother had thought the breeding of an Englishwoman would be sufficient for any situation. She had dismissed her mother's teaching regarding so much else, why had she not disregarded that? What an ignorant fool she had been.

Susannah put her head on the pillow. She was far more of a child than Intlack. Why had Simtlack thought she could be a Teacher? What a jest! Intlack saw far more clearly than did she! He had been honest enough to tell her he would regret her passing. Regret! That was the most anyone here would feel. And why should they care more than that for such a pompous idiot! She groaned, pulling at the pillow, wishing she could escape from her own brain. Would that she could awaken to the roll of the ship and her father's voice. At least if she died she could be with her father again.

Or would she? Suddenly her easy abandonment of all religious practices seemed stupendously important. She had been such a selfish creature, doing only what pleased her. Mocking her mother's pretensions, avoiding her father's dark moods, taking Chiang's help for granted and scoffing at his worries. Why had he missed the party? She would have to ask him … if she ever got the chance. So self-centered she was! What Supreme Being would want her? Driven to it at last, she rolled to her knees and said the first true prayer she had said in years: *If you are there, God, please send me some help.*

Things didn't look any better when she woke. She still felt that she was a worthless creature who might as well be killed immediately. She tried to wallow in despair for awhile, but she couldn't. She knew there would be an answer to her prayer. She knew it. Was that foolish optimism or faith?

When there was a knock at the door, she held her breath. Knowing it was ridiculous, she pictured a priest outside — one of those Jesuit missionaries she had occasionally seen during her travels. Her mother had always warned her against them, believing them to be agents of the devil. Her father had admired them, saying they were fearless, no matter who they worked for. Susannah knew they could be found in all sorts of unlikely places — why not here? Eventually she realized that whoever had knocked was waiting for permission to enter. She cleared her throat, feeling silly, and said, "Please come in. Walk into my parlor," she added a little hysterically, "said the spi—"

A tree shuffled slowly into her cell. A tree with branchy looking feet and arms and stick hands, and a rough, weathered, dark brown face. Around the face was a lot of stuff which looked like lichen, and above the head were branches and leaves which scraped the ceiling. Susannah and the tree regarded each other in silence, for a moment, and it seemed to her that the tree's amber eyes looked into her soul.

"Are you hungry?" asked the tree at last in a slow, calm, we've-got-all-the-time-in-the-universe voice.

Susannah closed her mouth, then opened it. "Yes." It seemed the polite thing to say.

The tree pulled something which looked like an apple off of itself and handed it to

her. "Guaranteed wormless," it said, big brown lips cleaving into a smile.

"What is it?"

The tree's eyes widened. "An apple!"

She bit into the apple, and the crunch of her teeth echoed the sound of the tree's lips. She slurped to catch all the juice. She nibbled all the way to the core.

The tree seemed pleased and planted its large feet widely, as though settling in for a century or two, and wriggled its arms and branches and shook its hair and beard. Wisps of lichen drifted to the floor. "Ahh! That's better. We have much speaking to do."

Susannah started to put the apple core down, but the tree held out a large hand. She put the core into the hand, feeling the rough texture of it, smelling fruit and forest.

The tree disposed of the core somewhere inside of itself. "No thing in the universe ever ends completely."

Susannah's unquenchable curiosity was rising — like sap, she thought, unable to stop herself. "May I inquire who you are?"

"I am Morabalateerashimistan. You, being of a species of short patience, may call me Morabal."

"What manner of creature are you? If you do not mind my inquiring?"

"I do not mind your inquiring of me any thing at all. I am, in the speech of my home world, called by a word which would take so long to say that you would sleep and wake several times before I had finished. Therefore, you may consider me to be a tree." Morabal winked a very slow wink. His eyelids shone smoothly with a beautifully swirling grain.

Susannah found herself blinking rapidly, as if her eyes wished to emphasize the difference between them. "Why have you come to me?"

"A soul in pain cried out to me."

"Are you a — a priest?"

"This is a name I am not familiar with."

"A religious person?"

The big face wrinkled. "I am not sure that I —"

"Are you one who feels exceptionally close to God, or the Almighty, or the Creator, or whatever you may wish to name

Him, and who feels compelled by that belief to share your faith with others — regardless of their desire to hear?" Susannah stood up and paced impatiently around the room. "Are you one who tells others what they should and should not do?"

The tree sighed, a gusty breeze, smelling of peaches. "So many contrary explanations." There was a pause, as though Morabal had to grow the answers to her questions. "We are all close to God, as you call it. We all pay attention to that Being in our own ways. We all do as we must. We —"

"I think you must be a priest or a minister. You speak circles around the question, but you speak too slowly to be a philosopher."

The tree's great lips cracked wide again. "I speak slowly, young woman, because I am a tree. It is my nature to be slow. Just as it is yours to interrupt, being so quickly impatient, ripening in the excitement of life."

Susannah sat down with a thump. She was being unbearably rude and the tree-creature was not getting angry. Her mother would be appalled at this treatment of a visitor.

A visitor to my cell, Mother! Susannah screamed in her head. *Leave me alone with your admonitions on my etiquette. Good manners have been of no use to me since Father died, and they are certainly of no use here!*

She shook her head, trying to clear the memory of a drawing room in England, and her mother sitting, criticizing, with a teacup in her hand.

"I would prefer less excitement in the present circumstances," she snapped. Then she straightened up abruptly as something occurred to her. "Have you come as my confessor? Because — because I am to be executed? Is this my final confession?"

The tree sighed again, and the branches shook, and the leaves rustled. "So many thoughts in such a hurry." It paused carefully. "I do not know of any killing. I came because I felt a need. Do you have a need to confess?"

"Ahh! Incontrovertible truth! You are a priest!" She stood up again and turned her back to the tree as she paced the two steps to the wall. Then she whirled around and paced back, slamming her feet down as she came. "I requested assistance of God." The words burst out of her, unbidden. "I suppose I should have expected a demand for confession." She glared up at Morabal and was fascinated by the drawing together of his enormous, scraggly, pale green eyebrows.

"I make no demands of you." The big head shook ponderously. "I am here because I felt a need. What do you need?"

Shame overwhelmed her. Morabal had made no demands. She had brought up the subject of confessing, and she was angry about it. Because she did have things to confess. And she certainly did not want to admit that to herself, still less to some alien creature. She put her hands up to her face, shaking, grasping for control.

"Release."

She turned her back to him, throwing her head up, gulping through a tight throat.

"*Release!*" His voice was like the crack of a huge branch breaking.

Susannah's control snapped with it, the storm breaking on her full force. She put her hands up to her face, trying to contain the flood, but the salty water poured through her fingers. She was dimly aware of creaking and rustling behind her, then something soft touched her tight, wet fingers. An enormous, brown hand appeared before her. It held a mat of lichen before her face. She stared at it uncomprehendingly, sobbing and gasping. Morabal turned her gently around. The tree wiped her face with the lichen, then drew her carefully against its rough, scaly trunk. The tears continued to flood. A few leaves drifted down on her as the tree patted her gently, making soothing rustling noises.

She cried for what seemed years. At last she pushed herself away and swiped at her face with the lichen. She blew her nose and took a deep breath.

"Yes," she choked out. "I do have things to confess." The words brought on another storm, a gale of guilt and self-pity. Morabal waited. When she was calm again, Susannah began to talk.

She began at her beginning and talked, and cried, and ate apples, and talked some more until she had reached her apparent end. Morabal listened. She looked up at the tree with a small, damp smile. "I have told you everything about myself, and I do not even know if you are a male or a female tree."

The crevice of Morabal's smile appeared. "That does not matter even to other

trees."

Susannah's eyes widened, but she decided not to pursue that topic. She smiled. "Why do I feel better? My circumstances have not changed."

"No?"

"I am, of a certainty, no better a person than I was before you entered. And I am still a prisoner."

"You are not as bad a person as you were telling yourself you were before I came in."

"Am I not?"

"Are you?"

Susannah smiled. "You are a philosopher. You pose many more questions than you answer."

"I do not know 'philosopher.' But I do know that questions are good for the soul. The one who has all the answers soon begins to pay too much attention to the perceived faults of others."

She thought about that. "What questions do you have?"

"Are you as bad a person as you were telling yourself you were before I came?"

She laughed again, feeling free. "You will not allow me to evade you again."

"No. I will wait until I know you have answered for yourself. You do not need to tell me. I will see it." Morabal settled back on big feet.

Susannah looked down at her hands and tried to speak lightly. "Indubitably there are people who have greater faults than I."

Morabal startled her with a thunderous roar: "*Beware*! Judge yourself by your own inner standard only, Susannah Rebecca Chambers McKay! Comparing leads only to dissatisfaction, either with yourself or with others. What should you be?"

"I–I am sorry." Susannah chewed her lip. "Intlack and I spoke of that one day — judging others. But I find I have no standards for myself. I have only ever been taught to compare." She looked up at the tree beseechingly.

"I cannot tell you how to be Susannah. I only know how to be Morabalateerashimistan — and I am still becoming that." Morabal stretched out long branches and rustled them. "But you are asking the questions now. That is good. You see that you cannot be a good or bad Susannah without a scale to judge by. That is a fine thing to learn." Morabal pulled up first one foot and shook it, then the other. "It is time." The tree turned with snappings and crackings toward the door. "I assist with services every day for anyone who wishes to attend. Will you come?"

"You are leaving me?"

Morabal smiled. "Some questions are best explored in silence. Will you come?"

Susannah looked up into the amber eyes. It was so different from looking into Snactyl's eyes. Morabal seemed to see into her, and to gently hold what was found, encouraging growth. "I would be delighted to come — if I am able."

"Perhaps you would like these?" A few apples were held out to her.

"Thank you!" Morabal turned ponderously toward the door. "Morabal!" The tree turned back with no sign of impatience. "If they should resolve to — to execute me — would you accompany me?"

"As far as I am able." Morabal shuffled out.

Susannah stared at the door. Her thoughts seemed both clear and obscure. She felt compelled to do something, but it was very confusing to her. This would be only the second real prayer of her life. The first had been answered rather promptly. Was there really a God? Did such a Being really listen to her? And if so, why? Why? The answers were not forthcoming, but the impulse was still there.

Feeling awkward and silly, she knelt. "If You are in existence, and You are listening to me," she paused, swallowed and continued, "I am sorry for all I have done which may have offended You. My life has been full of wonders — especially lately — and I have shown little appreciation." She stopped to work up her courage. What if this prayer were answered as swiftly as the other? Did she really want this? "Please ... please help me to become a better person. And — if it is not too much trouble — give me some time to do it. Please let me live." She sat down on her pillow and tried to hope.

11.

S USANNAH WONDERED if her new found peace would last
when they took her to be killed. She was certain now that
they would kill her. She could think of no reason why they
would not, particularly after this long imprisonment. She
wondered just how long it had been ... After awhile she tried to
sleep, but she had not learned how to get comfortable with her
new thoughts. She also kept burping up apples.

She was beginning to feel rather lightheaded when the
door opened suddenly. Chiang slipped in, carrying a large
bundle. "I don't know what you said to him, but Intlack ordered
that you be given some clean clothing, and I talked Thorty into
letting me bring them to you." He threw down the bundle.

She raised a dazed face to him. "Oh, Chiang, thank you!
Thank you! And, Chiang," she reached a hand up to him, "please
accept my sincerest apologies for the way I spoke to you before.
I am most deeply sorry for my behavior since coming aboard. I
have made your assignment so much more difficult than it ought
to have been."

He stared at her. "Don't you want to put on your clean clothing? You're a mess."

Susannah was delighted to find that she felt no anger at this blunt statement.

Perhaps she really had changed already! At any rate, it was true. Her lovely party dress was torn and streaked with swamp mud, and her hair fell in grimy tangles down her back. "It does seem pointless without bathing first," she sighed.

Chiang grimaced. "I'll try to arrange it."

"Oh, no! I did not mean that! Please do not do anything more for me. You have done so much already! And I have made it so hard for you."

He frowned at her suspiciously. "Why are you talking like this?"

"I am expressing my regrets."

He shifted and would not meet her eyes. "That's not necessary."

"It is for me. Whatever happens to me, I wish to have a clear conscience." She

said it so calmly she surprised herself.

And she astounded Chiang. "A clear conscience?"

"Is the concept foreign to you?" She caught her breath. "Forgive me. I have little practice at holding my tongue. But I intend to work at bettering myself. For as long as I am able."

"As long as you are able ... Ahh! I think I begin to see. Confession and atonement. I remember a missionary who converted many people in my village ... long, long ago." He leaned against the wall. "Well, if you're going to try to be polite, I will try to enjoy it. though I am not sure which is worse — your former incivility or your present false humility."

"False! False!" She sat up straight. "I am not given to falsity, you —" She snapped her mouth shut. He was grinning. "You did that deliberately. Well. I cannot deny that it will take time for me to unlearn unfortunate tendencies. Time which I may not have —"

Chiang straightened up angrily. "What is this, a farewell speech?"

"In a manner of speaking. I did tell you, I want to apologize—"

"For what? For taking on a job I offered you? For trying to find out information which I should have given you? For getting into trouble at a party to which I should have accompanied you?"

"Please do not blame yourself," she said gently. "I do not."

"Ha! Spare me your high-mindedness! I have as much right to confession as you do." He squatted down on his heels and leaned toward her, his brown eyes brilliantly hard. "Do you know what happened on my first ship? No, of course you don't. It's one of the many things I never told you. Maybe if I had, you would have acted less like a child on holiday. I was recruited to be the assistant to the secretary of a diplomatic family. Not Shill — another species. Not so important, not so rich, and not so tolerant. They chose me, because they happened to be near Earth when the former secretary was killed, because I have a facility for languages, and because their scans showed I was capable of learning quickly. Also, like you, I had no relatives to notice when I disappeared.

"Again, like you, I jumped in feet first, so certain of my ability to adapt, so thrilled to have this — opportunity!" He spat the word out. "Too late, I found out I was a virtual slave, as had been the assistant before me, in a system closely resembling the feudal system of your Great Britain's history. My predecessor had the bad judgment to try to escape and had been killed.

"The person put in charge of my orientation was considered to be totally responsible for me. So when I messed up — and I will never tell you the details — she was put where you are sitting now. And killed. And I was given her job." He looked as though he were about to be sick. Susannah did not dare to say anything. "The only good thing about that was that in the course of my duties I managed to impress Simtlack, who more or less requisitioned me. Simtlack's views are a little more enlightened than my previous employer's. He is holding you responsible for your actions rather than me." He stood up, and she could see the tears in his eyes. "You go to hear judgment tomorrow." He left.

"Judgment," whispered Susannah. "And I forgot again to ask why he missed the party."

•   •   •

Susannah dreamed she was asleep on her father's ship; in her dream she was dreaming, and in her dream within a dream she saw an angel. The angel was the rather severe Michael pictured in the stained glass of the church her mother had favored. He held up a sword with one muscular arm, and he watched with apparent satisfaction as his brother Lucifer plunged into Hell. Susannah had always wondered how a brother could be glad to see a brother fall. She had always preferred the picture of Raphael playing his lute in the window opposite. But Michael was the one who appeared to her.

"You have asked to live." He didn't have his sword, but his voice was as sharp and deeply slicing. Steely dark eyes peered down at her, unimaginable knowledge shining in them.

"Yes," she whispered.

"Why?"

"Why?"

Michael nodded sternly, and his wings rose and fell with the movement of his head.

"I value my life! Life is — desirable. Am I not supposed to value it?"

The angel's long robe shimmered. "Not everyone does so."

That reminded her of the window in the church: the black shine that was Lucifer, falling into the glowing orange and red glass that was hell's fire. Susannah burst out, "Why did you not grieve for your brother? Have you no family feeling?"

Michael's wings flew up and his eyes flashed the silver of his sword. "You question me?"

"Yes." Susannah quaked in her bed.

Michael smiled. His smile was fierce and terrible. "Young woman. You will make a fine warrior for the Lord. But you must learn to pick your battles and know your opponents. For your first battle, I give you this advice: Do not defend yourself. You don't know your opponent."

"But — I thought you said I was to be a warrior."

"A warrior must have forbearance." He gave her a regal nod and his wings swept wide. "And know this as well — you have not yet earned the right to question an archangel." He flew off into a stormy sky, and a crack of thunder woke her from her dream within a dream.

Her father was bending over her.

"Oh, Papa, I have missed you so!"

Her father patted her gently. "Take the risk, me darlin'!" He laughed and his laugh turned into the shriek of a seagull. Her father the seagull flew into the air.

"But, Papa! I need you alive!"

"No one dies who chooses life, me darlin'!"

She woke up crying, because he had flown away.

•　　　•　　　•

Sometime later, the one Chiang had called Thorty delivered a small tub with several large, wet sponge-like rectangles. Susannah gave a cry of delight. As soon as he was out the door, she stripped off her filthy clothing and cleaned herself. The large sponges seemed to contain an unlimited supply of a damp cleanser which smelled lovely and took care of the worst of the stains. It felt so wonderful that she risked taking her time, although she was worried Thorty would come back before she was done.

When she was sure she was as clean as possible, she put on her new clothing (all pale gray) and sat to wait. She need not have worried about being interrupted. She had more than enough time to think about seagulls, angels, trees, and life, and to wonder whether she should take the dream angel's advice seriously.

Eventually Snactyl came for her. How the snake opened the door, Susannah had no idea. Susannah saw no one but Snactyl, slithering in and trying to pin her with those eyes. Susannah faced the snake, keeping her eyes averted, and said, "I am ready."

"I am ssincserely ssceptical of that." The snake swayed her long form back and forth as though she heard music.

Susannah took a firm grip on her newfound convictions. "I know you do not like me, Snactyl, but if I have offended you in some way, I am sorry."

"Sss sss." It took Susannah a moment to realize the snake was laughing. "I ssusspect you are! I am a dangerouss creature to offend, ass you now ssee!"

Susannah sighed. Snactyl would never believe she was sorry for any reason other than self-interest. "Lead on, MacDuff."

"SSss?"

"Show me the way. Please."

The snake turned and slithered out the still open door. She paused in the corridor for Susannah to join her, then slithered at her side until they reached a doorway curtains in red. They went through side by side, like the best of friends. The courtroom was circular, with a platform in the middle. There were no spectators. The only creatures present were ones she knew. Witnesses, she supposed.

And Morabal was also there, she was relieved to see. When she met the amber eyes,the tree winked. Susannah took a deep breath and strode firmly up to the Family aligned on the platform. As she came to a halt in front of them, she saw that the Creeks were also there. Their dull gray hides were hard to discern. Susannah wondered how they found status with the Shill. Then Snactyl encircled her, and she suppressed a shudder as the snake's head hovered waist-high at her left side.

[You have been apprehended while spying,] Simtlack rumbled. *[You have been convicted. Do you have anything to say?]*

Susannah gasped. "I most certainly do! What do you mean, convicted? You have not visited me! You know nothing of my viewpoint!"

[You have seen Snactyl. And Snactyl has seen me.]

"On my world it is customary for the accused to face her judge when being tried!"

[This is not your world, human. A point which you seem to have a great deal of difficulty remembering. You have been convicted by your own actions. You are seeing me now. What have you to say?]

Susannah opened her mouth — and closed it. She remembered clearly the angel's words: Do not defend yourself. *Then what am I to do?* she wailed inwardly. They kept telling her this was not her world, but … "On my world, it is customary for the accused to have someone to speak for her." She fought to keep from squeezing her hands together, to keep her words calm and reasonable.

[This!] bellowed, Simtlack, and Susannah stepped back a pace, almost treading on Snactyl, *[is not your world!]* He stopped suddenly, and his tentacles swiveled toward Cheetlon. *[I am Shill. I can attempt to fathom/tolerate/endure barbarian ways.]*

Why are the accused on your world unable to speak for themselves?

"The accused are often fearful and unfamiliar with the ways of the courtroom. As I am. Another speaker, a speaker whose fate does not rest on the result, is believed to be better able to think and speak rationally."

Simtlack's tentacles pointed at the ceiling a moment. *[There is nothing complex about our judgment procedures. And you appear rational to me. However, it is with strength that I say, I will be merciful/indulgent/magnanimous. Whom do you wish to have speak for you?]*

Susannah drew a deep breath. She thought she might be able to hug Simtlack one day. Even as the thought crossed her mind she was glad she had a shield which hid it from Simtlack. *Now what do I do?* she wondered, desperately scanning the room. She saw Chiang watching her. He thought she would choose him, but his eyes showed his hopelessness. Susannah looked away. She saw Morabal. The tree's eyes widened, and it rustled uneasily. Susannah almost laughed. She winked at the tree and looked on. Dory's tiny hands grasped her afghan close. *She is frightened for me,* thought Susannah. Then she remembered the rest of her dream. Her father had said, "Take the risk." What risk?

Susannah saw Intlack on the platform next to his father. He knew her point of view. He was not hopeless or frightened. He was young and alien. That was the risk she would take.

"I choose Intlack."

Intlack's tentacles pointed at her. She could see the tension in his neck. She shook her head hastily. She saw him suppress the outburst he had been about to make. She wondered at herself — able to gauge the feelings of this snail-child. She wondered more at the pleasure she felt on seeing Intlack's self-control.

Simtlack moved toward her. Susannah was startled to feel Snactyl contract, as though the snake wished she could abandon her position. Snactyl, afraid of Simtlack? Belatedly, Susannah remembered what Intlack had told her about the pain Simtlack could inflict. She strove to hang on to the tatters of her nerve.

Simtlack's tentacles came within touching distance of her face. She had never seen them so close before. They were far more captivating than Snactyl's eyes. They were a brilliant emerald, rapidly darkening to a deep, dark green. She began to feel a twinge of pain, then sharp pressure, then a fierce, hot stab; the pain was so great that she fell against the snake. Snactyl, hissing, slithered away from her, and Susannah sprawled on the floor, moaning.

Intlack slid forward. *[Father. I wish to accept the Teacher's request.]*

[Why?]

[We brought the Teacher here, Father.]

[We?]

[We Shill. If she is unfamiliar with our ways, it is our responsibility. It is not the fault of the Teacher that she is slow to learn of us properly.]

[Should we then blame her Teacher?]

[No, Father. She is our responsibility. I confess that I wondered why you summoned her ... Her species is notoriously impulsive.]

Susannah held her breath, wondering why she was able to hear this discussion,but grateful that she could. Whatever came of this, she could not be sorry for having some part in the education of this young creature.

[Have you come to some conclusion, my son?]

[I have concluded that her request is reasonable.]

Simtlack was silent. His tentacles pointed toward Cheetlon, and this conversation, Susannah could not hear. However, after a moment he said merely, *[Very well.]* And he backed away from Susannah. Speak.]

Susannah sat up and then slowly rose to her feet, staring at Intlack. Now that he could do so, it was evident did not know what to say. She held her breath.

[The Teacher claims to have not been spying.]

[The Teacher was seen in the swamp.]

Susannah stared at Simtlack. She got the distinct impression that he was enjoying himself now.

[The Teacher claims to have entered the swamp to avoid Snactyl.]

Susannah felt Snactyl's movement just behind her, but the snake did not take her earlier position, nor dare to interrupt.

[Why should an innocent avoid Snactyl?]

[The Teacher claims that Snactyl frightened her. Snactyl attempted to probe her. We know that Snactyl's probing can be — crude. To a weak-minded human it seems terrible.]

[So. That does not explain spying.]

[The Teacher claims that to avoid Snactyl she attempted to cross the swamp.]

[Cross the swamp?]

[The Teacher did not know that this was our meeting place.]

[Why did she not know this?]

Chiang stepped forward. "It was my duty to inform her. I intended to do so at the beginning of the party, but I was — indisposed."

[What sort of indisposition was this?]

Chiang swallowed. "I had had too much ziltlur."

Simtlack looked at Chiang for a moment. *So that's what happened,* thought Susannah. *He was getting inebriated before the party.*

She considered Chiang thoughtfully as Simtlack continued: *[This overindulgence in spirits must stop.]*

"Yes, sir."

[Continue, my son.]

[The Teacher thought she could walk to the other side of the swamp, rejoin her friends, and Snactyl would not find her.]

[Snactyl not find one for whom she was looking?]

[We know the Teacher is sometimes foolish and has an undisciplined mind.]

[True.]

Susannah sighed.

[When the Teacher came upon our meeting place, she attempted to withdraw. She slipped and fell in the mud.]

[Much clumsiness.]

[You have seen her stumble over Snactyl.]

[Yes.]

Simtlack's tentacles turned in the direction of the Creels. They burled and burped like cauldrons on the boil. Simtlack looked at Intlack. *[The crucial interrogative is: what did she hear?]*

12

I NTLACK WAS SILENT for a long moment, and Susannah shuffled restlessly. Snactyl shifted and Susannah glanced at her. She was faintly amused to see the snake looking apprehensively at Susannah's feet.

Intlack said at last: *[The Teacher did hear something.]*

The Creels gave forth a few flatulent pops and a sour, swampy smell wafted through the room.

[I will relate to you and Mother only, the words heard by the Teacher.]

For an endless time, Susannah waited, the courtroom silent but for the Creels' burbling. Susannah tried to get Chiang to meet her eyes, but he would not. His face looked damp. Was it sweat or tears?

Simtlack stirred at last. *[I will discuss with the Creels.]*

Susannah shuffled her feet. Snactyl's tail twitched. Susannah looked at the faces of her friends. Morabal's amber eyes met hers calmly. She tried to soak in some of that patient waitingness. She remembered suddenly a part of a Bible passage she had learned as a child: To everything there is a season. The tree epitomized that. A time for every purpose under heaven. Did that hold true when one was in the heavens?

Simtlack's voice startled her out of her reverie.

[We have determined that what was heard was nonessential.]

A breath of a sigh passed through the court. Susannah stared at him, barely daring to hope.

[The Creels wish to be undoubting that that is all she heard.]

[The Teacher has told me only of that, said Intlack firmly.]

Simtlack's tentacles swiveled. *[Snactyl?]*

"The Teacher hass a mind sshield. Why?"

Simtlack's tentacles swiveled back to Intlack.

[She did not appreciate/suffer gladly having her surface thoughts known at all times by us.]

She asked the Dorian to help her, and the seamstress complied. The seamstress has exceeded her role.

[She is a Dorian, old, and occasionally interfering.]

Cheetlon made her first audible comment: *[I was aware the first meeting time of the Teacher's discomfort with our ability to know her so easily. I believe it is not uncommon for the human creatures to feel so. Chiang has long had a mind shield.]*

[Chiang has proven his loyalty. I would know why my son, the Eldest, is so assured that his Teacher imparts Truth.]

[The Teacher has shown me to the best of her ability all that has occurred. I hear Truth.]

Snactyl hissed, "The Eldesst iss inexperienced. A clever sspy can create surface thoughts on the mind which obsstruct the true."

Simtlack considered. *[Teacher, please show for us your memories of the night.]*

The Creels burbled.

[It matters not what she reveals. I will ensure that only Snactyl, my Consort and the Eldest hear. And your gracious selves.]

He bowed toward the Creels, then turned to Susannah. *[Begin.]*

Once again, Susannah went through the events of that night. She forgot that she stood in a courtroom as Simtlack prodded her, pulling details out of her brain like threads from needlepoint. She saw again the dancers, felt her drink fizzing on her tongue, smelled the swamp as she shrank back out of Snactyl's view. When it was over, she was surprised to find herself in clean clothes, swaying tiredly in front of the platform.

"The human'ss sstory hingess on sso much clumssiness and sstupidity! Iss anyone sso foolish?"

Intlack was silent as his father's tentacles regarded him. *[Well, my son?]*

[I ... have witnessed other ... examples of the Teacher's inadvisable actions and awkwardness, Father. I was angered/ humiliated/distressed the first time I spoke alone to the Teacher. She was so unwise/outspoken she accused me of rudeness.]

Oh, Intlack, thought Susannah. *Please do not do what I think you are considering. It is not worth it. I am not worth it.* She shook her head at him.

[You spoke of examples in the plural tense?] asked Simtlack.

Susannah desperately shook her head.

[Yes. There is one. But I cannot speak of it.]

"No!" whispered Susannah, taking a step forward. Snactyl hissed and slithered toward her.

[Cannot speak of it? What is this?]

[I cannot speak of it. I should not think of it. Yet, because of it, I am convinced of the Teacher's innocence. I can say no more.]

"I cannot accssept ssuch a sstatement."

Susannah hissed at Snactyl and the snake hissed back.

[Nor can I. You must elaborate, Eldest.]

[Yes, Father. This concerns a nihilism.]

"No!" cried Susannah.

[Intlack!] cried Cheetlon.

[Intlack!] bellowed Simtlack. Then he was silent for what seemed to Susannah to be several years.

"No, oh, no," she whispered to herself.

Finally Simtlack spoke, his thought-voice was choked: *[I say your name no more.]*

Desolate wailing emitted from Intlack.

[You are no longer my son. You must —]

"*No!* This is ridiculous! You cannot do this!"

Intlack's head rose and he shook it desperately.

[What?]

Susannah clapped her hands to her head at the pain of that shriek of fury.

"Susannah!" Chiang leaped forward. "Don't! Haven't you learned anything?"

"Yes! I certainly have!" She deliberately trod on Snactyl's tail and marched up to Simtlack.

Snactyl reared back, but by then Susannah was standing too close to Simtlack for the snake to do anything. "I have learned that you have a valiant son, Simtlack! Why have you not learned this? You were forcing the truth from him! Will you now deny the truth you hear?"

[Be silent, Teacher. He has spoken of the forbidden. He must leave his shell.]

His wailing a low keening, Intlack began to crawl out of his shell.

"Stop right there, Intlack!" Susannah put out her hand and touched Intlack's bare neck. Shocked, he stopped. Susannah looked Simtlack in the tentacle. "All my life I have done what I believed was best for me! It took this son of yours, who appears to me to be a slimy worm, to teach me about self-sacrifice and responsibility. I do not know why you brought me here, Simtlack. No one seems to comprehend your choice but you! I do not know if I have taught Intlack one thing. But I do know that Intlack has been a Teacher to me! And he could be a Teacher to you, if you would only listen. You said you had the strength to listen to a barbarian. Do you have the strength to listen to your own son?"

She faced him, hands on hips and high on adrenaline. "You have a perfect right to throw me in prison or blast my brain, or whatever it is you do, but you have no right to abandon that — that courageous young Shill!" All her righteousness used up, Susannah stepped back, looking at Intlack, still frozen where she had stopped him.

She heard a rustling behind her and assumed it was Snactyl come to apprehend her. But it was Morabal who stepped to her side.

"It appears your plan worked, my friend."

[Pardon?] Simtlack lifted his tentacles.

"Your son is a powerful and merciful diplomat, just as you hoped."

[My son — my son is lost to me! Outcast!]

"Achh!" the tree barked. "You do not really intend to invoke that old chestnut, do you?"

[What other can I do? The law is clear.]

"The law also states clearly that you must use any opportunity to develop Eldest offspring into diplomats worthy of the Empress. I do not think she would appreciate seeing such potential lost."

[He cannot be aware of a nihilism! I was not!]

"Come now, Simtlack. Do you not remember a time when you had to force yourself to not-think of a nihilism?

[Well ... Perhaps.]

"Yes. And how can you expect the creatures around you who have not your training to always remember to be unaware of a nihilism? Yet, they are disallowed from speaking of it to you without imperiling their lives! Nihilisms made sense when only the Families and their servants were involved — but now you encounter many, many weaker minded ones, and true nihilisms are no longer possible. This is a law which needs adjustment, Simtlack."

[You have been my Teacher for a long time, Morabal. And you are always after me to change something. How do you propose I untangle this development?]

"I do not know. I am not the diplomat — you are. A powerful and merciful diplomat who makes concessions out of his strength. Do your job." The tree put a huge gnarled hand on Simtlack's shell. "It is right that you do this."

Simtlack's tentacles wove back and forth. He consulted with Cheetlon. He came to a decision. *[Is my courage any less than my son's, whose valor is great, as the Teacher has said? I brought you here, Susannah-Teacher, because you come from a society which deems itself superior to those around it. I had seen a similar attitude in my son. This disturbed me. A diplomat must be more powerful than his urges, more merciful than his strength requires, and more open to new ideas than the rest of his society. I believed that you would be a negative example to teach him the error of his ways. I apologize. I used my power inappropriately, and I misjudged you. You have been a Teacher to all of us.]* He bowed his head.

Cheetlon moved up beside him. *[Simtlack, speak to your son!]*

[My son. My pride in you is more than I can express. Return to your shell and to your place at my side. I declare nihilisms are no more in this quadrant. The Teacher is pardoned.]

Intlack edged backward into his shell, but he was apparently, speechless.

Cheetlon projected joy. *[We have much to be thankful for. Morabal will help us to express this to the Master at services tomorrow. This court is to empty.]*

Simtlack, Cheetlon and Intlack formed a tight circle facing one another.

Susannah looked at the Creels. They burbled their way out, but whether they were satisfied or merely too in awe of Simtlack to complain, she did not know.

Snactyl slithered up to her side, and she took a step backward. "You have nothing to fear from me, human. Ssimtlack hass pardoned you. That iss final. I am ssorry if I have missjudged you, ass you have missjudged me. Chiang hass told me of Earth's creation sstory. I am not an evil being, though I am a ssnake." She slithered away.

Susannah stared after her, astonished.

"Susannah." Chiang's brown eyes reflected his relief. "I am sorry I was not at the party, and —"

"Oh, Chiang! You have nothing to be sorry for! Did you not hear Simtlack? He employed me to be a bad example. And I certainly was that, was I not?"

"You — you — Will you never learn to take things seriously?"

"I certainly hope not!" She wanted to hug him, but she did not know how she could. "Thank you for being my friend."

He shook his head. "With friends like me ..." he muttered, and walked away.

Susannah watched him, wondering if they would ever achieve simple friendship. Intlack broke away from his parents and approached her.

[You risked your life for me.]

"Not really. I was already convicted. You did risk all for me, however. Thank you."

[Why did I do this?]

"I think because we have grown to love each other."

[Mating/reproducing/Family?]

"No. Caring/valuing/friends."

[I have never had a friend before. And you are not Shill. You are a barbarian!]

Susannah smiled. "Perhaps it is possible for even the unShillvilized to be worthwhile friends."

[Perhaps. I will think on this. We will discuss it tomorrow.]

"Yes, Eldest."

Intlack turned and slid away. Susannah smiled. He left a trail of slime behind.

ABOUT THE AUTHOR

Susan McDonough-Wachtman has been writing since grade school. She has tried her hand at children's stories, short stories, romances, historical novels, essays, fantasies, mysteries, science fiction, numerous letters to the editor, and a blog.

Susan has been a burger tosser, customer service rep, ad taker, curriculum developer, parent, teacher, reader, and gardener. She lives in the Pacific Northwest with one cat and one husband.

Most recently, "Mother, May I" was accepted for the Halloween edition of *Tales From the Moonlit Path*, "Xanthippe" was included in a Brigids Gate anthology, "Pantsed" was published in *Willow* magazine, and "I Will Go Gently" appeared in *Metaphorosis*.

YOU MIGHT ALSO ENJOY

BUILDING BABY BROTHER

Steven Radecki

It seemed like a good idea at the time ...

CHILDREN OF THE WRONG TIME

Flavia Idà

"Would you say you were loved by the right people at the right time in the right way and for the right reasons?"

POSSESSION IS NINE-TENTHS

J Dark

Possession might be 9/10th of the law. But no one mentioned 9/10th of what.

Available from Water Dragon Publishing in
hardcover, trade paperback, digital, and audio editions
waterdragonpublishing.com

www.ingramcontent.com/pod-product-compliance
Lightning Source LLC
Chambersburg PA
CBHW051232210726
48290CB00003B/928